The Matchbox Dragon

A. J. Webb

To Dear Rose Best Wishes Always
Andrew

Bloomington, IN   authorHOUSE®   Milton Keynes, UK

AuthorHouse™
1663 Liberty Drive, Suite 200
Bloomington, IN 47403
www.authorhouse.com
Phone: 1-800-839-8640

AuthorHouse™ UK Ltd.
500 Avebury Boulevard
Central Milton Keynes, MK9 2BE
www.authorhouse.co.uk
Phone: 08001974150

This book is a work of fiction. People, places, events, and situations are the product of the author's imagination. Any resemblance to actual persons, living or dead, or historical events, is purely coincidental.

© 2007 A.J. Webb. All rights reserved.

No part of this book may be reproduced, stored in a retrieval system, or transmitted by any means without the written permission of the author.

First published by AuthorHouse 11/1/2007

ISBN: 978-1-4259-9187-6 (sc)

Printed in the United States of America
Bloomington, Indiana

This book is printed on acid-free paper.

Cover illustration by A.J. Webb and all other illustrations by Tom Simpson.

Dedicated to all my friends and family.

Chapter 1.
The Thunder storm.

It had been an ordinary day for young Alex Wood and the school day had passed without any major dramas. Little did Alex know that by the end of the day his life would change forever?

Mum and Woody, the family's pet black Labrador, had come to meet him and his older brother Tom at the school gates. Now this was Woody's favourite time of day and his doggy senses were on full alert, sniffing all who came in range of his shiny wet nose. His tail was constantly wagging as he patiently waited for the boys.

However Woody, always the opportunist, could not resist checking out school bags and pockets for edible goodies while he was being petted by his adoring fans. Everyone loved Woody and he loved them back.

Today was the last day of term before the summer holidays. And it was with an air of excitement a stream of children spilled from the swing doors and up the short driveway towards their waiting parents. At last Tom and Alex emerged chatting and laughing with their school friends as they walked towards an excited Woody and smiling Mum.

"Had a good day boys?"

"Yes Mum," was the reply as they both hugged her in turn.

Woody's tail was in overdrive as he smiled in his own doggy way circling the boys and nuzzling in on the welcome. His lead wrapped around their legs as Tom and Alex knelt down to make a fuss of him. Both boys tried to avoid his welcoming wet tongue but Tom caught a particularly wet kiss. He stood up disgusted, "Oh Woody!" he whined.

Mum and Alex laughed as Tom wiped his cheek then ran ahead to join a friend who had just walked by.

"Come on then Alex lets get on our way," said Mum directing Woody to her side.

Mum, Alex and Woody headed off towards home following Tom on the pathway beside the school road. They joined the throng of other parents and children all carrying satchels and rucksacks crammed with homework and empty lunchboxes.

This was a quiet road normally, but it was now lined with a host of waiting 4X4s and people carriers. It was a beautiful sunny afternoon and the prospect of the coming summer holidays were infectious. Many of the children laughed and giggled as they walked playfully along the path by the side of the road. Happily they waved goodbye to their friends as the doors on the queues of school run cars opened and closed.

All swallowing their lively cargo's in succession like hungry Hippo's on a river bank.

True to form Woody held up proceedings, stopping to pee on the front wheel of what happened to be the headmaster's car, much to Mum's embarrassment but to the delight of the children who cheered and giggled at Woody's natural and innocent action.

Within minutes they had left the houses and roads behind them and were walking on a winding path that led through a wooded green quite close to where the family lived.

Alex spotted a few other boys and asked his Mum if he could stay a while and play. She agreed and relieved Alex of his school bag and other paraphernalia.

"Come on Mum!" said Tom, tugging at her arm. He was itching to entrench himself in front of his computer at home.

"Now Alex, make sure you are back home for tea at five o'clock and please don't ruin your school clothes."

"Yes Mum. Thanks Mum," said Alex and he scampered off to join his friends.

Mum and Tom crossed the field and disappeared through a gate in the hedge followed by Woody who stopped and sniffed at every available opportunity.

Alex and his friends were soon taking it in turns to swing on the rope hanging from one of the high branches of big oak tree that dominated the clearing.

They played all sorts of games, running with the football circling its vast trunk under the shade of its canopy. This huge oak was hollow and the boys used the opening to its heart nicknamed 'the witches hide' as a goal. Of course retrieving the ball was turned into a spooky dare as the boys scared each other with tales of ghosts and strange monsters, which might just be hiding in the dark centre of this ancient tree.

Time passed very quickly as the boys played in the late afternoon summer sun. Finally after an energetic and noisy kick about Alex checked his watch, it was nearly five. "I have to go now!" he shouted.

He gave the ball coming towards him a last mighty kick and waved good-by to his friends "See you later," they said.

Alex ran home as fast as his legs could carry him. Bursting in through the kitchen door, grubby, hot and his shirt hanging out, he could see tea was on the table.

It was fish fingers and chips, one of his favourites.

He was almost about to sit down when Mum interrupted him.

"Alex wash your hands and look at your knees!" she said, shaking her head.

"And look at those shoes too!" she added with disgust pointing at his feet.

Alex gave Mum his practised cow eyed forgive me look, then carefully removed his shoes and placed them by the back door. Then after washing off his muddy hands in the kitchen sink he plumped himself down at the kitchen table. "Pass the tomato sauce Tom please," He said. Tom duly obliged and Alex squeezed the plastic bottle making farting sounds as he squirted the sauce on his food. "I don't know," Mum muttered as she placed two slices of bread and butter on the saucer by Alex's plate. The boys giggled and carried on eating their meals but this harmony was not to last for long.

Tom noticed Alex had one of his trading cards in his top pocket and the usual argument ensued between the two brothers. It was nearly always over who owned what pencil or toy, but possession was nine tenths of the law as far as Alex was concerned and a mini tug of war broke out over a Yu-Gui-Oh trading card.

Mia the boys' older sister also seated at the table had been daintily eating a salad. She just rolled her eyes at Mum in disgust.

"Stop it you two, you are supposed to share," said Mum sharply.

Tom finished his tea in silence, then got up from his seat with a glum look on his face and disappeared to his bedroom.

Alex and Mia helped Mum clear the tea things from the table, and within a few minutes the task was done. Mia then took up her favoured position outside under the garden parasol and was busy texting friends bathed in the afternoon sun.

"Thank you for helping Alex," Mum said as she wiped some tomato sauce off his top lip with her apron.

"Sorry about the shoes Mum," Alex said sheepishly.

"Go on, away with you," she said as she gave him a little hug.

Alex felt like a quick game on his PC. So he headed off up stairs followed by a shout from Mum to brush his teeth and change out of his school clothes.

This dutifully done, Alex sat down in front of his computer and clicked on to his favourite race car game. He had worked hard on the cars specification keyed in on his PC, and was well pleased with the result held in the computers memory.

Now it was a race to destruction in the carefully chosen and built virtual race car.

After an hour or two of racing and crashing, Alex sat back in his chair and yawned.

He had a busy day and as he stretched, Mum came in, "OK young man its time for bed." Alex slipped his pyjamas on and a kiss and a cuddle followed as Mum tucked him in.

"Off to sleep now," she said and gave him a final kiss on the forehead.

"Night Mum," he said as she disappeared through the door.

Dad wasn't home yet but Alex knew he would look in on him whenever he got home, even if he was asleep. Alex yawned and stretched under his duvet and although quite sleepy, he felt he wanted to have just one last look outside. So he climbed out from under his bedclothes, knelt on the end his bed and looked out of his bedroom window.

He could see from what had been a very hot sunny day, big black clouds where creeping in from the horizon. The huge swirling cotton like shapes loomed towards him like a giant moving mountain range. He knew instinctively that a thunderstorm was on its way.

Creeping back under his duvet again, he waited. It was growing darker as the wind blew the heat of the day away. The first heavy drops of rain pattered on the window thrown against the glass by the increasing gusts. Suddenly a flash lit the bedroom; he gripped the duvet tightly and froze.

Babb- BOOM , crackle, sizzle, babbooooom--- his room shook, and just for just that moment he was a little scared. Alex wanted to climb out of bed and run downstairs to his mum.

But he remembered that his dad had told him not to worry; it was just the clouds bumping together. So with one eye open and the covers of his duvet held up to his nose, Alex watched the approaching storm through his bedroom window.

The rain was now falling so hard it was bouncing off the roof of the house, the foggy mist it produced fell off the gutters like a waterfall in slow motion.

All the elements of the storm gathered now as the skies grew even darker and gusts of wind increased throwing the droplets of rain like tiny stones against his window.

Another flash lit up the sky and the lightning jumped from cloud to cloud like a giant jagged spider's web. Alex braced him self for a huge bang, but all that followed was a kind of sizzling crack, followed by a long distant boom.

Then, just as suddenly as it had started, the torrential rain stopped and the wind released its grip on the flaying trees. It was if a giant switch had been thrown in the heavens and all natures' energy had been spent.

Somehow Alex felt compelled to watch the storm being chased away by the evening sunshine. So slowly he emerged from the safety of his duvet and soft pillow. He climbed out and knelt on the end of his bed again. Looking out through the window again he could see blue sky and sunshine racing towards him chasing the menacing black storm clouds away. He leant forward and opened the window a little and within minutes as he watched, the power of the Sun transformed the garden below into a steaming jungle. At least dad won't have to water his plants tonight, he thought.

Alex opened the window a little more and leant his head out; and there to his amazement on the window ledge was what he thought was large winged insect.

He was just about to poke it with his finger when it moved. He pulled his hand back so quickly he banged his elbow on the window frame, "ouch!" he cried.

"That was a silly thing to do," said a tiny squeaky voice. Alex froze as his senses took in this strange apparition. The tiny creature then uncoiled and turned over.

To Alex it looked just like cross between a newt and a seahorse with wings. He was transfixed and fascinated at the same time by this unusual creature. Had it really just spoken to him?

Alex's jaw had almost dropped to the floor, and then he started to babble.

"What are you? Where did you come from? How did you get here?" completely missing the point that a talking creature had just spoken to him.

"Well cool" he aspirated, as he gently poked the little creature relaxed and drew his breath.

The little animal then spoke again, "Yes that's just the point" pausing and looking at Alex. "I was washed off my mothers back by the heavy rain, could I come inside and dry off?" "I really am very cold."

"Of course," said Alex, still cautiously studying this strange talking insect. He carefully reached out and the little creature climbed onto his hand. It actually felt quite hot.

"Thank you," it said, as Alex placed it on his bedside table.

"I'll get some tissue paper to dry you off" he said, racing off to the bathroom.

Alex pinched himself on the arm while looking in the bathroom mirror, just to make sure he wasn't dreaming.

Just then Mum shouted up the stairs "are you OK Alex?"

"Yes Mum," he said, "just going to the loo."

Running back with a hand full of tissue he sat on the bed and carefully mopped and dried the little creature. "You are not a newt are you? I've not seen one with wings before," said Alex.

The little creature opened one of his wings and blew over it, trying to disperse some of the droplets of water remaining on its greeny black finely scaled skin.

It then settled into a position rather like a cat sitting on its haunches. Alex was fascinated by a long pointed tail wrapped around the front, the end of which was waving gently like a tiny snake.

"No, I am not a Newt, or an insect, my name is Dolphis and I am a Dragon!" declared the creature proudly.

Alex a little surprised but now quite calm said, "But I thought dragons were enormous?"

Dolphis sighed and looked at Alex. "We were once millions of years ago and there weren't that many of us even then. Those of us that where left have been hunted by so many beasts, that only the very small ones that could hide, have survived."

Dolphis drew a slow breath and continued. "Today we are so small in size and numbers that you don't even know we are here, and of course we have the power of a chameleon so we are very difficult to see."

"Cool, that's really cool" said Alex again, still amazed, and struggling to find something to say. "Well-- my name is Alex Wood and I am seven years old. I have an older brother and a sister and--."

"I am sorry to interrupt you," said the little creature, "but I am really cold and I if get too cold I will fall ill."

"Right!" said Alex leaping up. "How can I help you?" Dolphis looked around Alex's bedroom, "that little box over there looks quite cosy."

Pointing with his tiny front right claw, to an old matchbox, "but it must be lined with something that won't burn."

"What!" Said Alex "OK err-- don't worry I think I have just the thing."

Luckily several chocolate bars had been consumed over the last few days and the wrappers were still in the bin in the corner. The silver paper was carefully extracted, then Alex folded and placed it carefully in the match box, adding a little lid several layers thick. "Is that OK?" said Alex.

"Perfect," said Dolphis as he climbed in and tried it for size. "Ooh it's a bit of a squeeze but that's really quite comfortable," said the little Dragon now smiling weakly.

Wondering what else he could do. Alex asked "Are you hungry, what do you eat?"

"Coal," said Dolphis, and a little snack would be nice, I am feeling a bit hungry."

"COAL!".... Exclaimed Alex. Thinking to himself, we are all gas and electric here, where am I going to find some coal? There was a pause as he racked his brain. "I know" he said excitedly, his mind thought back quickly to the barbecue at the weekend, "would charcoal do?"

"That's fine," said Dolphis "but only just a few tiny lumps, that's all I need."

"Right" said Alex. Slipping on his tea shirt and thinking quietly to himself again.

How on earth am I going to sneak past Mum, the dog and of course his brother, and down into the garden at 9.30 at night.

Dolphis then made another request; "Alex, I can tell by my keen senses--- that small black box near the floor," pointing to an electrical socket, "is really quite warm."

"Yes that's my game consul transformer" said Alex.

"If that's what it is then, I think it would keep me at just the right temperature, please could you put me and the matchbox on top of that?"

"No problemo," said Alex and he gently slid the matchbox draw shut with the little Dragon inside and placed the box carefully on the warm transformer.

"See you in a minute," he said as he slipped his trainers on.

"Thank you," was the muffled reply from inside the box.

Alex still gave no thought to the fact that he had just talked to a dragon, almost is if it was an every day experience. Gathering his thoughts together he stood with his hand on the handle of his bedroom door.

This was going to be tricky; he needed to get into the kitchen and out the back door leading to the garden. He eased open his bedroom door and carefully edged towards the stairs. He could hear Thomas in his bedroom rattling the keyboard on his computer, probably conquering another world or playing some game of ancient warfare.

And hopefully his sister Mia in her own bedroom was probably oblivious to everything. Busy texting some spotty boy or equally obnoxious girlfriend from school.

But Woody the Labrador was another matter. Once his tail starts to wag, walls, doors, furniture, everything. It is all beaten by his wagging tail with the vigour of a base drum, and would announce his presence for sure.

There was only one thing for it, hope that Mum would be watching a tennis match or something. Perhaps with Woody chewing his favourite toy at her feet, only an earthquake would shift them from that.

I'm just going to have to take a chance, I hope I can remember which of the stairs the creaky ones are he thought. Ok here goes, and he crept out onto the landing.

Carefully he crept down the stairs with just the odd creak slowing his progress, and stealthfully he peered around the first corner.

Phew! The coast was clear, so far so good he thought. Carefully and quietly he continued to creep ever downwards, the hall was in sight and woody was absent.

He could hear the bink bonk of a tennis match coming from the living room, he breathed a sigh of relief. What luck he thought, just as he had hoped.

Easing across the dimly lit hallway to the kitchen door, he gathered himself together and smiled imagining he was just like James Bond on a mission.

He had just reached the kitchen door and was about to open it, when woody barked several times from inside the living room, and a shadowy figure appeared at the front door behind him.

Alex turned round and froze the smile disappearing from his face as he heard the key turning in the lock.

The front door opened and there stood his dad. "Hi Alex what are you doing up so late?" Dad said, as he closed the front door behind him.

Alex's mind was going ten to the dozen, although pleased to see his dad, what would James Bond have done? And could he disguise the fear of being caught out on his first secret mission. Alex's shoulders dropped as he struggled to get out some words, but now he felt more like Mr. Bean. "Oh dad," he stuttered, "I was woken by the thunderstorm and I am just getting a glass of milk."

"OK sunshine," said dad, bending over him and kissing him on the forehead, "but don't be to long its way past you bedtime." Dad smiled at Alex as he opened the door to the living room and whispered, "See you in the morning."

Woody leapt out at dad with a doggy enthusiasm matched only by the meeting of a long lost relative at the airport, his whole black body unable to contain the excitement of welcoming his master home.

Eventually dad and Woody disappeared into the living room while Alex transformed himself back into Bond mode and slipped through the kitchen door like a fox on the prowl.

He quietly opened the back door and tiptoed over the lawn towards the garden shed, the mission target, inside which he had hoped to find a bag of barbecue charcoal.

But the shed was locked, blast he thought, what now? Then he remembered the actual barbecue itself on the patio, maybe there was a few bits of charcoal left on the grate?

This presented problems in itself as woody was now watching proceedings from inside the patio door, his doggy senses at full alert, but at least Mum and dad where busy chatting oblivious to Woody's antics.

It was now dusk and nearly 10.oclock. Being caught now would be an instant grounding. Only one thing for it, just do it.

Alex crouched using the size of the barbecue to hide behind and hoped he would not be spotted, his hand went up and fumbled in the cold grate but most of this was soft ash.

Ah! what's this?...... His fingers felt a piece of unburnt charcoal at last.

Dolphis said he did not need much, this will do, he thought.

Retrieving several small lumps and placing them in a little tin box he had found in his toy box. Alex then headed back across the moonlit lawn towards the kitchen door.

Safely back inside the kitchen he cracked open the door to the hallway, he could hear Mum and dads muffled voices discussing the days events.

"Fhew.."….. He exhaled and wiped his brow with the back of his hand. Cautiously he continued to negotiate the unlit hallway and quietly tip toed his way back up the dark stairs.

Now back in his bedroom and quite relieved he turned on the bedside lamp. To his surprise a pair of very black hands were in evidence, he hurriedly looked around to see a few more fingerprints on the lamp and bedroom door.

Panicking slightly and now with the light on, he glanced through his bedroom door to the other side of the landing, and there to his horror was a black trail of incriminating evidence, splodgy black marks all up the stairs. And worst of all, on the newly painted walls, perfect black smudgy hand prints spiralled down towards the hall. Oh my god he thought, he was dead meat, and he would be grounded for a month at least.

Pausing and thinking for just a moment…. Panic mode now set in. I've got to get this mess cleaned up, I have to wash my hands, and he blindly dashed to the bathroom. Splish, splash the bathroom sink was now black. Splish, splash, black spots and streaks were now everywhere. Even the towel was about to be treated to a black marbled effect as he hurriedly tried to wipe the incriminating evidence away, but it was all just getting horribly worse…… Mum and Dad would go ballistic.

In all this pandemonium Alex had forgotten Dolphis and the reason the whole house was seemingly turning black. He just did his best to clean up himself and the surrounding area. Dejected and solemn Alex returned to his bedroom and went down on all fours by the electrical socket the transformer was plugged into. He was just about to lift the matchbox off the transformer when he heard a sort of intermittent buzzing sound. Dolphis was fast asleep. Alex smiled weakly and realised, he too was exhausted; Oh hell….. he thought I'll just have to face the music in the morning.

He gently slid open the box and watched the little dragons chest rise and fall as he snored contently, quite oblivious to the drama.

Alex sighed and dropped in a few grains of the hard won charcoal picked out from his little tin box, then whispered, "Good night Dolphis" he thought, Dolphis?

That could be a boy or a girl; I'll ask in the morning. Alex yawned several times, then climbed into bed and fell quickly into a deep sleep.

Chapter 2.

Keeping the secret.

The next morning came; and Alex had slept to nearly 9 o'clock. He sat up in bed rubbed his eyes and looked over at the matchbox resting on the transformer.

Had he dreamt it all? Why wasn't Mum breathing fire and brimstone at him in his bed? He leapt out of bed, gently picked up the box it was open, and it was empty. Looking round his bedroom there was no sign of a Dragon or indeed the black dust. With a sigh he thought, it must have been a dream and scratched his head in disbelief.

Oh well tennis lesson this morning best get ready and have some breakfast.

Just at that moment his Mum shouted upstairs. "ALEX! Breakfast!"

Still in his pyjamas Alex walked through the bedroom door onto the landing, it was all coming back.

Where are the black hand prints? Puzzled he shook his head again.

He wandered sleepily into the bathroom and there to his horror was the towel, hanging there as black as the ace of Spades, and yet everywhere else was spotless. What was going on here?

Even more puzzled, he thought to himself, I must have been sleep walking or something. I'll get a clean towel out of the airing cupboard and sneak the black one into the washing machine later.

Sleepily Alex then opened the airing cupboard door, and to his absolute delight there was Dolphis, curled up as snug as you like on a fluffy blue towel, but with a tummy as big as a Japanese wrestler.

Dolphis stirred and stretched. "Oh good morning Alex," "that charcoal you left for me last night was delicious. I climbed out of the box to stretch my legs and it was all over the place, I just couldn't resist it. It was just like the best food you could have ever tasted." Dolphis then burped quite loudly for such a small Dragon, and went on to say disappointedly, "but I just couldn't face the towel."

Alex gaped at the little Dragon for a few seconds then almost burst with excitement. "Dolphis you are my hero! You've saved my life," and said with a big grin on his face. "So I wasn't dreaming after all. Look I have to go off now, are you ok in here?"

"Not half," Dolphis smiled back, "that immersion water heater must be running at about thirty degrees centigrade and I could do with a longer sleep." Dolphis let out another loud burp and a hiccup as he coiled up in the soft towel and closed his eyes.

"See you later," laughed Alex, and he sped off down the stairs to breakfast as happy as can be.

An hour or so later after his tennis lesson, Alex returned and rushed up stairs to see his new found friend. He opened the cupboard door but to his dismay, neither the towel nor Dolphis where any where to be seen.

Alex panicked for a moment lifting up the towels and hunting every corner of the airing cupboard. He stopped to gather his thoughts and there drifting from the bathroom he could hear the cheery whistling of dad and the sound of the shower running. Oh my god, he thought, of course, dad, shower, and towel.

He slipped into stealth mode, tiptoeing up to the bathroom door across the landing like a silent predator stalking his prey. The bathroom door was just ajar and he could see the blue towel lying on the floor.

Dad was busy behind the obscured glass door of the shower humming and whistling like he always does. I will have to be quick, thought Alex; dad could finish at any moment. He scratched his head and in a flash his plan was hatched, simple, change the towel.

With the speed of superman he was back at the airing cupboard and on his way back to the bathroom with another towel. But before he could get through the door, the shower was turned off. Dad stopped whistling and the shower door was opening.

Alex leapt in and stood between Dad and the towel on the floor. Quickly he lifted up the substitute towel while dad was still rubbing his eyes, and before dad could say or do anything, Alex spoke, "There you are dad let me pass you the towel."

Dad put the towel to his face while Alex bent down and as carefully as he could he picked up the blue towel.

"See ya later dad" he quipped and walked out the door as cool as a cucumber, leaving a slightly bemused dad thinking that, perhaps he was still dreaming.

Alex wasting no time scuttled off to his bedroom, grinning, and clutching his prize.

Bouncing onto his bed Alex carefully unwrapped the towel, but Dolphis was nowhere to be seen. "Nuts," he muttered. He turned his head and looked at the matchbox, of course he thought, leaping off the bed.

He picked up the box and slid open the draw. His heart sank, it was empty.

Perhaps Dolphis had fallen from the towel when dad picked it up.

Oh no!! "Woody," he would just about eat anything that looked even remotely edible. His heart sank even further. Just then a little squeaky voice said "you can't see me can you he, he, he."

"Dolphis!" shouted Alex. Where are you?

"I was clinging on to the towel all the time" he said "I told you I had the power of a chameleon." Alex rushed back over to the towel on the bed. And Dolphis appeared as if by magic. "Cool" said Alex with a great sense of relief. "Am I glad to see you, I thought you where a gon'na."

"Alex," said Dolphis "you must not worry about me, although I'm still quite young for a Dragon, I'm very old in your human years, and I am really quite good at not being seen."

"Just the same Dolphis I was worried and you never told me how you came to be here?" said Alex, "and are you a boy Dragon?"

"Yes I am and I will explain it all to you."

The little Dragon settled down and took a deep breath and said in a stern voice.

"But you must promise never to say anything to anybody. Unless it's absolutely necessary or they will hunt us down and put the few of us that are left in cages and zoos. And we have to be free to work our magic."

"That's cool I promise, cross my heart." said Alex reassuringly.

"Well, we Dragons can only fly during thunderstorms, it's to do with positive and negative Ions," he explained as he stretched and flapped his leathery little wings. "Normally we live quite deep below the earths surface, where is really quite warm all the year round. Usually near a nice tasty coal seam," said Dolphis licking his lips.

"It is actually nothing for a Dragon to sleep for a several years after a particularly big meal of coal dust. But for flying we need to refuel frequently and use the lighting strikes on tall trees mostly, as refuelling stops. Do you follow me so far?"

"I think so." said Alex.

Dolphis continued "But now in the season of sixty four million and eighty five, there are only a few colonies' left throughout the world and meeting up with other Dragons is very hard indeed."

Alex stretched out on his bed rested his head on his hands, listening to every word with great concentration. "Go on Dolphis tell me more."

"Well we were being led by Drockfoss, the leader of our family, trying to search out a new coal seam in the hills, as ours had slowly flooded over the last few hundred years.

We of course had to wait for the right type of thunderstorm and although we can glide a little. We can only get high enough with the help of the almost invisible electrical particles. They sort of stream up towards the clouds and are then trapped by our bodies and wings. Are you still with me Alex?"

"Yes, yes" he replied still thinking what it must be like to live deep underground.

"But how did you come to be on my windowsill?" Alex asked.

"It was an accident really." Dolphis took another deep breath and continued. "My mother, whose name incidentally is Dolpher, was carrying me on her back and I had fallen asleep. Suddenly a huge gust of wind carried us way up into the storm clouds and we got blown way off course. I just got washed of by a sudden torrential downpour of rain and was carried inside the thunderstorm for miles."

"Luckily I glided down and ended up on your windowsill, cold, wet and of course would of just of died if you had not of helped me warm up. So thank you very much indeed Alex." Dolphis smiled a little dragon smile as Alex reached over and stroked the back of his head. "You know it is Dragon law that we are never to reveal ourselves to humans, unless it is exceptional circumstances. You won't let them put me in a cage will you?"

"Of course not," said Alex "I promise, and we must try and think of a way to get you back to your family somehow." "Let's shake on it."

Dolphis put his tiny clawed hand on Alex's finger and the deal was sealed. Now all they had to do was hatch a plan and execute it.

Both of them were now deep in thought, when suddenly Thomas burst through the bedroom door like a tornado. "Who were you talking to?" Tom exclaimed.

"Oh nobody," Alex said nervously, as he slid Dolphis carefully behind his back.

"Yes you were," Tom said.

"Oh, oh yes I was just practising a few lines for the school play out loud, that's all."

Alex knew Tom's attention span was very short, so he fired back. "How's your new game coming on?" Trying to put him off the scent.

Tom paused for a second, "Yea great," said Tom, "the Roman army have tried to attack my cities but I've held them off with my chariots and archers, but I am running out of supplies so I'm going to have to raid the next country with my reserve army in the north." Tom stopped and thought for a moment. "I guess I'll be getting back to it then." Tom spun on his heel and was gone as quickly as he had arrived.

Alex breathing a sigh of relief and looking round to see where his friend had gone, Said "Dolphis are you OK?" Dolphis suddenly reappeared as if by magic sitting on the duvet. He coughed, and little puffs of smoke shot from his nostrils taking the form of two yellow rings that got bigger and then vanished.

"I'm hungry," said Dolphis, "Oh and thank you for rescuing me from that steam room." Alex smiled and opened up the little tin box he had put the remains of the hard won lumps of charcoal in.

Dolphis sniffed the air almost as if it was the aroma of the finest roast dinner. "Ahhhh," he sighed, as Alex picked out a small lump and gave it to him. Without hesitation, crunch, Dolphis took a bite; chewed several times and licked his lips. "Mmmmm that is nice," he said, still chewing.

"As you can imagine Alex," he said, pausing to pick out a small piece of charcoal from between his teeth with his tiny clawed hand. "We Dragons are not made the same as you humans."

Alex Laughed "I can see that, do you drink anything?"

"Well not very often," said Dolphis, "the odd sip of coal tar now and again, but we do like a corn and vegetable oil brew. It's made only by the most senior of our elders. But we can get very drunk on it, if we have too much."

"Ok," you drink oil then." "Errrke!" Alex screwed up his face and poked out his tongue pretending to spit. "Give me diet coke any day."

The little dragons' eyes lit up. "Yep, we drink oil----, but! what's this coke stuff?"

"No, no, no," said Alex, "not coal type coke! This is a dark coloured fizzy human drink."

"Sounds interesting," said Dolphis with a mischievous smile.

"You can try some if you like, I'll get you some."

"OK," said Dolphis, sitting up on his hind legs getting excited.

"Don't move I'll be back in a second." Alex jumped up and sped off down stairs to the kitchen. In his rush he almost knocked over his sister as he swung round the stair rail post. "Alex!" Mia shouted "you almost knocked me over and busted my phone."

This fell on deaf ears as he ran into the kitchen, slowly followed by Mia carefully checking her phone over.

Hurriedly he looked in the fridge for the dark elixir. "Ah there's a can." Reaching in, he took his prize.

"Have you asked Mum?" Mia quipped in a sisterly bossy way.

But there was no reply from Alex.

"Humph," she said, flinging her head back and continuing to punch the keys faster than an expert Morse code operator. Another text was on its way.

Alex bounded back towards the stairs, squeezing past Mia with the can of cold coke dripping in his hand. He raced up the stairs and entered his bedroom where Dolphis was waiting expectantly on the bed, rubbing his little clawed hands together grinning in anticipation of the treat to come. Alex dropped down and kneeled in front of him and flicked open the ring pull on the can.

Whoooooosh, Dolphis was instantly soaked in cold coke. "Brrrrrrrr," said Dolphis as he rubbed his eyes. "Oh my god I'm so sorry," said Alex reaching for an old tea shirt on the chair. Dolphis licked his lips, "mmmmmm, this is quite nice," he said as Alex blotted him with the tea shirt. "You like it?"

"Mmm-- yes it sort of tickles your throat," Said Dolphis with a little grin on his face.

"I'll make you a little cup, now where's that silver paper?" Alex found some more silver paper and started to fashion a little goblet around his finger. "There you are," he said and proudly handed Dolphis the cup. "Fit for a king ay Dolphis?"

Dolphis gripped the tiny vessel in his two hands and smiled. "Thank you, come on then pour some out for me," he said, licking his lips. Alex carefully filled the miniature goblet and watched him sniff it, just like the wine tasters he had seen on the TV.

Then without a moment's hesitation Dolphis tipped up the cup and slurped the whole lot in one go. There was a moment of silence. "Well! What do you think?" "Are you OK?" said Alex concerned. Dolphis rolled his eyes several times, then sat up strait and let out a mighty burp. Flames and smoke shot out of his nostrils like two small blow lamps.

Alex sprung back in startled surprise waving his hands to clear the smoke while checking round to see if anything had caught fire.

Relieved all was Ok he just said "WOW Dolphis you're dangerous." Dolphis just slunk back on the bed looking a bit sheepish.

"Sorry about that," he said "I wasn't prepared for that," and he let out another small burp followed by a tiny puff of smoke. "There's powerful magic in that stuff," he said swallowing. "I feel quite light headed and a bit floaty too."

Alex sat up suddenly, looking towards the door. "I can hear Mum coming up the stairs. Quick hide under that," and he unceremoniously slung the tea shirt over Dolphis.

"Alex,"….. Mum said loudly, as she came through the bedroom door.

"Frazer's at the front door and---," she stopped in mid sentence, surveying the bedroom like a detective and sniffed the air. "Something's burning and where did you get that can of coke?"

"Err, oh, I, um, sorry Mum," he drawled, putting on his best, please forgive me look face. "That burning smell must be coming from outside," he said, pointing to the open window.

She moved over to the window and glanced out. "Yes it's probably your dad working on that old car in the garage." Satisfied she added, "About that can of coke."

"Alex Dearest," she said sternly, "you know you should always ask."

He desperately searched his mind for an excuse, but relented, and just said "sorry Mum."

"Ok," she said "just don't ask for any more today." She then bent down and started to pick up the various clothes scattered around the floor. "Right I'll tell Frazer you might go down for him when you've tidied up your bedroom."

"OK,"…… he said reluctantly.

Mum put her head on one side and said "come on then."

Alex swung into action as Mum turned round and went back down the stairs. Shouting back up, "I'll check your bedroom later, so do a good job."

"Yes Mum," he shouted back. Swinging round and looking on the bed, now where's Dolphis gone now? He thought.

Searching round his bedroom he spied the open matchbox on his bed.

Bathed in the hot morning sunshine he could just see the little dragon's chest rising and falling. Dolphis had found his way back to his temporary sleeping quarters, and was fast asleep in the matchbox. Alex picked it up, slid the draw shut and carefully placed it in his shirt pocket. He could feel the tiny vibrations of Dolphis snoring against his chest.

Alex smiled, placed his hand over the pocket and said to himself. 'Don't worry Dolphis we will find a way to get you home to your family.

Mean while, I think I will go down to the garage, and see how dads getting on, repairing Old No Eight.   I'll catch up with Frazer later.

Chapter 3.

The trip to Grandad's.

Old number eight was dad's vintage car, a 1930's MG two seater. It was once grandad's car who is just as potty about old cars as dad. Dad had always had some sort of classic car or motorbike project on the go, and this was his eighth, hence the name, old no eight.

It was a lovely sunny morning as Alex made his way downstairs and out to the garage at the bottom of the garden. As he got closer to the side door he could hear dad talking to his beloved car. "Come on old girl, let's give it a go."

Alex entered the door and there was dad, his head under the bonnet in greasy old overalls, with bits of rag hanging out of the pockets. Dad stepped back and stood up wiping his greasy hands on a rag. "Hi dad." said Alex.

Dad swung round sort of surprised. "Morning sunshine, you are just in time," rubbing his hand on Alex's head and smiling. "Jump inside and pull that knob with the S on it would you." Alex had done this before so he knew what to do. Alex leapt in the car, "ready dad."

"OK, ignition on and pull the knob," said dad. Kr Raa raa Kr raa raa raa raa raa,--- Kr Raa raa Kr raa raa raa raa raa.. "Hold it," dad said. The engine was turning over and dad was operating the throttle under the bonnet, but there was no sign of life. He made a few more adjustments with a screwdriver.

"OK!... go again Alex." Kr raa raa raa, Kr raa raa raa,raa, Kr raa raa raa raa raa,--- "Come on old girl," said dad, still opening and closing the throttle under the bonnet. "Nothing---- Hold it," dad said again. He stood back from the car staring at the engine bay, screwdriver in one hand the other scratching his head looking puzzled.

Alex automatically turned off the ignition. "I don't understand it," said dad, "I've checked it all over at least three times now."

Alex to his surprise heard a little voice from inside the Matchbox say, "Check the fuel lines."

Alex coughed to cover up the voice. "What was that Alex, what did you say?"

Alex coughed again, as he pretended to clear his throat, "Have you checked the fuel lines dad?" Dad looked at him kind of sideways and thought for a moment, then put his hand on his chin and said, "Yes mmm, I'll blow them through with the air line, it's worth a try, good idea Alex."

While Dad removed the fuel lines, cleaned and blew them through. Alex sat in the driver's seat sawing at the steering wheel. He was imagining he was racing at Brooklands duelling with the snarling monsters of race cars that grandad was so fondly always telling him about. Dad chuckled quietly to himself listening to Alex's vocal soundtrack as he replaced the fuel lines. Soon it was time to give it another go. "Right you are Alex do your stuff." Alex returned from his imaginary race and turned on the ignition.

Dad stood by the throttles as Alex pulled the starter button. Kr raa raa raa raa raa raa cough, spit, brroom, brroom, a staccato roar came from the exhaust along with a plume of blue smoke. "Hooray!" They both shouted over the noise of the engine. Dad smiled and gave Alex the thumbs up as he revved the engine.

Sitting in the driver's seat clutching the steering wheel Alex gleefully watched the rev counter needle dance up and down on the dial in the dashboard.

Imagining he was once again a racing driver waiting for the start of a race. "Switch her off please." dad shouted over the noise.

They were both so excited. And with the engine off, Dad reached over and patted Alex on the back, "well done son I'm promoting you to chief mechanic," Alex was beaming all over his face and muttered under his breath, "thanks Dolphis."

"We are going to have to take the old girl out now you know," said dad.

"I know we'll pop over to grandads, let's go and have a glass of squash to celebrate and tell Mum where we are going."

"Great," said Alex, beaming like a Cheshire cat as he leaped out of the car.

Now in the kitchen drinking their celebratory glasses of squash, dad pulled off his overalls and Mum fussed over Alex saying, "Take a coat with you in case it rains, and go to the toilet before you go, and make sure you put that seat belt on too."

Mum had got out her handkerchief and was still wiping Alex's face as he tried to escape. Eventually he broke free and sprinted off to the bathroom.

Safe inside and the door locked, Alex pulled out the matchbox and slid it open. Dolphis was smiling back at him. "How on earth do you know about cars and things?" said Alex.

"I can read your books you know! And I read one once called, Automobile maintenance. Very interesting," Dolphis mused. "And my great uncle used to say, a nice warm car engine parked up after a run… is a very good refuge on a chilly night."

The little Dragon chuckled and blew a smoke ring at Alex.

"Right" said Alex. "Come on lets go with dad to grandads, you will like grandad he's really cool."

"Sounds like fun." said Dolphis ducking back into the matchbox.

Alex closed the box and put it back in his pocket. "Are you OK in there?" he said, "snug as a bug in a rug," chuckled Dolphis.

Alex skipped outside to meet his dad by old no eight on the driveway. Mum was standing by the car smiling at dad. She gave him a peck on the cheek; and said "is that thing safe?

You be careful now." Dad laughed as Alex climbed into his seat, "let me strap you in son. Is that comfortable?" "Fine," said Alex.

Then dad climbed in, did his belt up, and looked at Alex. "Do the honours chief mechanic." Alex beamed again, switched on the ignition and pulled on the starter knob. Almost instantly the engine roared into life and settled down to a rhythmic tick over.

Dad checked over the instruments making sure all was well.

After tapping the fuel gauge he snicked the old MG into gear and slipped off the handbrake. "Off we go then," said dad, letting out the clutch.

With a roar from the engine and a little cloud of smoke they sped out of the driveway, waving to Mum as they headed out onto the quiet country roads.

The bright dappled sunlight of the morning shone through the trees and hedgerows as the intrepid pair sped along the winding, undulating roads.

It was almost as if time had gone back to the 1930's, with just the occasional reminder of our modern age rudely flashing by.

Old number eight was gently speeding the time travellers along the narrow roads, cutting through little unspoilt villages on their way. Both dad and Alex listened to the exhaust note echo off the walls as people happily waved at them, it was all most enjoyable.

So with the wind in their hair, they smiled and waved back to the passing villagers feeling like a pair of time travelling celebrities.

It was almost as if by magic the modern world had disappeared. Old number eight reflecting and transporting them to perhaps a happier and less stressful place in time. Alex was enjoying himself and sort of realised why people enjoyed running and rebuilding these old cars, it was good fun.

It wasn't long before they were turning up into grandad's driveway, the gravel surface crunching beneath the wheels as they drove slowly up the drive.

Coming to a stop outside the big garage doors at the front of the house, they both still had huge smiles. "That was brilliant dad," said Alex.

"In your words, cool," said dad undoing his seat belt and getting out of the car.

Alex had undone his belt and was still sitting in the car while dad circled it, checking for oil leaks and anything working loose on the old MG.

Alex put his hand on his chest pocket and whispered "all right Dolphis?"

"Absolutely fine," was the muffled reply.

Just then the garage doors swung open and there was grandad in all his glory.

His sparkling blue eyes and cheery smile was almost camouflaged by his big white beard and moustache. A red tea shirt hanging on his small frame had obviously seen better days and had the words MANY A GOOD TUNE emblazoned in white letters on it.

The old boys' two spindly legs emerged from a pair of worn khaki shorts, like a pair of old gnarled walking sticks, terminating in a pair of equally old leather sandals. All this was capped by a shock of white curly hair on his head.

Well! it was a bit like, hippy meets Father Christmas, but what ever he looked like, grandad had a heart of gold.

"My boys," he exclaimed, "good to see you. Got the old girl running again I see?"

Grandad had used the old MG as his every day car for more than fifty yrs, but had laid it up round the back of the garage some years back with a busted engine and very tatty bodywork. Dad took pity on it, remembering fondly the trips that he and his father had made in the old MG. Now she was as good as new again. The beautiful red bodywork and silver wheels, shining in the morning sunshine.

"Dam good job, first class, a real credit," said grandad with a look of glee on his face. Grandad hugged them both, and dad said "Yes with the help of Alex we cracked it."

"This calls for a celebration then," grandad said, clasping his hands together, "and I've got something to show you two as well. I've just made some ginger beer come on in."

They followed grandad through the wide old oak front door and entered the large hallway. His house was very old, all low beams and flagstone floors, a sort of ancient labyrinth with doorways going here and there. Dotted everywhere, there were strange mechanical objects, seemingly abandoned amongst the equally old furniture and odd works of art. There was even a suit of armour guarding the passageway to the kitchen. Grandad called it Boris and always patted it whenever he walked past it. I guess you could call him a bit of an eccentric.

Grandad had been retired for many years and had worked for the government on many, he would say "hush, hush" projects. Most of his time was now spent working on his old cars and inventing things. It was always fun to visit grandad, thought Alex, you never knew what would happen next.

The trio entered the kitchen, dad and Alex pulling out the chairs and sitting round the big pine table. Grandad went over to the enormous old fridge, and opened the door. "Here we are my boys," he said gleefully, as he lifted out a large glass pitcher full to the brim with his home made brew. Gently he placed it on the table and got three large glasses out of the cupboard.

Carefully he poured his freshly made ginger beer into each glass. "Look at that," he said smiling, "my special recipe, it's what keeps me young."

Every one picked up a glass "Cheer's!" they all said in unison, and without further a due the refreshing drinks were all downed in one go. "Ahhh!" they all retorted, as the empty glass's returned to the table. A few seconds past, and they all burped one after the other, almost as if it was some strange initiation ceremony. "Ah that's better," said dad.

"Just the stuff to wash the flies from your teeth eh Alex," chuckled grandad.

"Awe grandad how could you," said Alex spitting something off his top lip.

Dad then stood up and said, "One of the front brakes was squeaking a bit on the MG, I'll just go and check them out."

"Help your self to tools son," grandad shouted after him as he disappeared through to hallway back to the car.

Alex somehow now knew that grandad was the man to help him in his quest to reunite Dolphis with his family, and he braced himself to broach the subject.

"Grandad" he said slowly, "can you keep a secret?"

"Brrr-rrrr" he cleared his throat. "Of course I can, I've signed the official secrets act you know." He said proudly twiddling his moustache.

"Well, I have an unusual friend who needs to get back to his family."

"Do you now…" he said in a low voice. Standing upright and putting his hands on his hips he waiting for Alex to reveal his secret.

Alex thought for a moment then leant his head down towards his pocket and said. "OK Dolphis, what do you think?"

"Fine by me," came a tiny reply. Alex reached into his pocket and fetched out the matchbox, placed it on the table and slid open the draw.

Grandad's eyes nearly popped out of his head as Dolphis emerged from the matchbox. The little dragon stood on his hind legs, bowed and said, "Good day sir."

"Well, well, by all the saints, I thought I'd seen it all," said grandad in a semi state of shock.

Alex went on to explain the whole story to grandad, who listened in almost stunned silence transfixed by Dolphis and Alex's story.

"Can you help?" said Dolphis. "Mmmm of course, of course old chap and my lips are sealed." Grandad spun round on his heels scratching his head, still a little stunned and quite taken aback by Alex's new friend. "Leave it to us my good man, err I mean dragon. I have an old book some where that might be just the ticket." Grandad composed himself and scuttled off muttering, still scratching his head.

Alex looked at Dolphis and Dolphis looked at Alex. "Grandad will know what to do," said Alex nodding confidently and smiling at Dolphis.

"I'm in your hands now my friend. And by the way can I try some of that ginger beer?" "NO!" Said Alex, "You know what happened last time."

"Oh go on, please," Dolphis said grinning in an appealing way.

"Oh all right then just a drop." Alex dipped his finger into the pitcher and held it in front of Dolphis's nose; the drop was sucked in with a little slurp.

"Mmmmmm this is even more powerful than that coal juice, I can tell. This could just be the fuel I've been looking for," said Dolphis with a big smile on his face.

"Fuel what do you mean fuel."

"Food, I meant food," Said Dolphis, going back on his words.

"Mmm always thinking about your stomach," said Alex poking Dolphis in the tummy.

"No more for the moment, we will check it out with grandad in safe conditions.

I don't want grandads house burnt down," he said sternly, trying not to laugh.

"OK point taken." said Dolphis. So a little disappointed he shrugged his shoulders and climbed back into the open matchbox.

At that moment grandad came back in clutching a dusty old leather bound book. "Look at this." he said dropping it on the table in a cloud of dust.

"Great, grandad," said Alex coughing on the dust, "how will that help us?"

"Well it's an account by Sir James Simpson Long, a famous mountain climber in the 1890's. He climbed many the peaks and mountains all over the world. And I seem to remember that somewhere in that book, on one of those mountains in Wales; he got terribly lost after losing his compass. He claimed he was guided down by a Dragon," Grandad said looking at Dolphis over his glasses.

"Everyone thought he was bonkers or even just plain delirious. But it might just be the clue to your homeland we are looking for, young Dragon." The old man winked and smiled at the pair of them.

"I have some old maps and all the bits and bobs we would need but I will have to do a bit more research."

Granddad paused and ran his fingers through his beard. "You know Alex I don't know whether its fate or coincidence but it just so happens I am off to see your uncle Nigel in Wales tomorrow." He paused again, "there is something else though," he added. "We are going to need to know the weather patterns for the last few days, you know, which way the wind was blowing and that sort of thing." "We are going to need some one with computer skills."

"TOM." Said Alex and Grandad both at the same time. "Can I leave that to you then Alex?" "Yes," he said with a little apprehension. "I'll get on to it as soon as I get home."

"Oh and yes there's something else, we are going to need a hand to operate my special sort of satellite navigation kit while I drive. Do you think Tom and Mia could help us out there too? As it is such short notice."

Alex's heart sank, Tom was one thing, but Mia, just getting her off the phone would be a miracle. "I'll help you, don't worry," said Dolphis, and he rested his little head on Alex's arm. "That's the ticket," chirped grandad, "you leave the rest to me."

"Now come on, I've got something to show to you and your dad before you go, and don't worry I'll clear everything with headquarters (meaning Mum and dad) before we go anywhere."

Grandad scuttled though to the hallway and shouted "BRIAN" that was dads name.

"Come down to the old barn in a minute, I've got something to show you."

"Right O." was the reply.

Grandad came back to the kitchen, collected Alex and Dolphis and they made their way through the kitchen to the big old barn at the bottom of the garden. The barn covered in shrubs and vines, blended in perfectly with the surrounding countryside.

Walking round to the courtyard, grandad produced a huge old key from his pocket which was attached by a chain to his belt.

They stood in front of the big barn door and he placed the key in the lock and turned it, Cer chunk went the lock.

"Ok Dolphis I need you to enter your voice into my personal entry identification system. Just in case your voice or presence sets the alarms off."

"What shall I say?" he said as he climbed onto Alex's shoulder.

"Just your name is fine," said grandad lifting an old leather flap on the door revealing a keypad and slightly rusty old microphone.

Alex leant forward to get Dolphis closer to the microphone and grandad pressed the red button 3 times. Grandad nodded towards the microphone and Dolphis took a deep breath. "Dolphis,Origmil,Loreum ,Pilmeum,Hinidume,Islormic,Somineu," he said smiling confidently.

There was a short silence as grandad and Alex looked at each other, and then burst into laughter, poor Dolphis was nearly shaken off Alex's shoulder.

"Sorry Dolphis," said Alex, still trying to hold back the laughter.

"That's Ok," dropping his head and looking a little sad, saying my name made me think of my family." Alex sighed and gave Dolphis a caring stroke. "Right," said grandad, trying to change the mood "On with the job in hand. And he spoke into the microphone. "Open ses a me." With a clank and a whirring of motors the great barn door started to open, they all stood back and stared into the darkness. Alex squinted and could just make out something car shaped under an enormous dust sheet.

They could hear dad coming down the garden path so Dolphis went into chameleon mode on Alex's shoulder. "Come on in." said grandad, switching on the lights.

Alex and dad had of course been in grandad's barn/come workshop many times and along with all sorts of strange machinery, recognised the many cars and motorbikes in varying states of repair. But what was this under the dust sheet?

"It's not?" said dad. "Yes." Beamed grandad, as he pulled the dust sheet off.

Proudly he revealed a huge monster of a car with shining British racing green paint work. Written on the side of the car in small white letters was "SPITTY."

"Corr! Granddad," said Alex as he walked up to it and leant his hand on the front cycle wings.

"Yes she's beautiful isn't she, built by me and my old mate Nigel in the 50s on an old Bentley chassis. She's got an eight litre engine you know and a supercharger." said Grandad, obviously very proud of his past handy work. "The chap we built it for past away recently and he had no family. He left it to us in his will just as he said he would all those years ago, bit of a surprise really."

"She's all ready to go. I've checked her out on test and am going to take her over to Nigel's in Wales tomorrow."

"Nigel and I have entered the Westfarland sprint/hill climb, a nice run of around 60 miles to get there." "Brian, why don't you and Jenny follow up as back up car in the MG? I'll take the kids in Spitty."

"Please, please, please, oh please dad can we go, please," Alex wailed while jumping up and down beside his dad almost pulling his shirt out, forgetting that Dolphis was clinging on his shoulder for dear life. "Its fine with me and I don't think Mums got any plans but there are other people to consider here," said dad as he put his hand on Alex's head to keep him still. "Yeaaaaaaaaa" Alex exclaimed.

"Come on chief mechanic lets get home for a late lunch," said dad with a smile on his face. "Dad," said Brian I'll phone you later."

"Right O," said grandad.

Brian tucked his shirt in and started to walk back up the garden towards the house.

"Alex here a minute," said grandad, holding him back. "Alex, Dolphis," whispered grandad, "The gods of fate and luck must have been on our side today. I think Westfarland hill climb is pretty close to where old Simpson-Long got lost all those years ago. So don't worry we will get you back home some how young Dragon."

"I will get everything prepared by tonight. And don't forget Alex, I need Toms weather info."

"We won't, thanks," they both said in unison as Alex gave him a little hug.

"Off with you now," said grandad, as he turned Alex around and patted him on the head.

"Just one thing Dolphis piped up, can you bring some of your ginger beer please?" "Never go any where without it," he said chuckling. "Now off you go I'll be there in a sec."

"Come on Alex get your skate's on," dad shouted from the top of the garden.

"Coming," was the reply as Alex slipped Dolphis back in his matchbox and into his pocket.

A few minutes later they where back in the old MG and ready for the off. Alex started the engine on dads command, and while Brian was turning the car round he shouted, "Phone you later Pop."

They all waved frantically as once again they headed off towards home along the narrow country roads in the midday sunshine.

Although enjoying the journey, Alex was now deep in thought wondering how he was going to recruit his brother and sister. Dolphis had fallen asleep again and Alex could feel the tiny vibrations of his snoring in his chest pocket.

He smiled to himself and was sort of excited at the prospect but he still had a lot of work to do. Little did he know what adventures lay before him?

Chapter 4-

Dolphis goes High tech.

Arriving back home and pulling back up to the garage, dad turned the engine off and said to Alex, "she's running like a dream but I'll give the old girl a good check over, just in case." Just then Mum came out stood by the car with her hands on her hips and said. "What time do you call this then?" It's a good job grandad phoned me to say you had just left, or your lunch would be in Woody by now," Mum laughed and added, so what's this about a trip to Wales tomorrow?"

"Yes love," dad said sheepishly, "should be good fun, are you up for it?"

"I am, she said but Tom and Mia are another matter."

"Leave that up to me Mum," piped up Alex.

"Oh you're a miracle worker now are you," she laughed.

"That's right," Alex said as he scampered towards the house.

"I'll make up some nice picnic baskets then," she shouted after him.

Back in his bedroom and sitting at his desk Alex started to think about the task ahead as he pulled out the matchbox and opened it. Dolphis yawned as he climbed out.

"What's the plan then?" he said sleepily.

"I guess I'm just going to have to ask Tom straight out." said Alex.

"Come on then," said Dolphis climbing onto Alex's shoulder. "No time like the present." They made their way to Tom's bedroom door, they could hear the familiar sound of battle cries and army's marching into battle. "I can't do it Dolphis," said Alex, pausing at the slightly open door, "Tom can be real ornery sometimes."

"Don't worry Alex I'll help too," said Dolphis reassuringly.

"OK let's go for it then." Alex shuffled through the door and stood beside Tom who continued to tap out orders to his army. "What do you want?" he said curtly.

"Tom I need your help."

"I'm busy," he said without stopping or looking round.

"Tom I really, really, really need your help."

"Go and ask Mum, I'm busy," he said impatiently.

"Oh please Tom it's your help I need."

As he spoke and to his amazement he saw Dolphis's image materialised at the bottom of Toms computer screen, and starting grow bigger and bigger. Tom's jaw dropped and he was frantically pressing the escape buttons on his keyboard, but he could do nothing to stop this apparition. "Oh my god my computers got a virus," he said panicking trying to turn off his computer. Dolphis by now had completely filled the screen and his image then started to speak, but not in a little squeaky voice, but a big powerful Dragon type voice. "I am the most powerful King of the high mountains to the west," boomed Dolphis, "and I will hold your army's under my spell until you have fulfilled the task your brother in arms has requested."

Finishing with a huge roar, and shooting a great plume of fire and smoke across the screen. Dolphis Digitally melted Tom's battle plan. "Hey!" Tom cried.

"You have a problem?" boomed Dolphis's apparition sternly.

"No, no, no, what do you want me to do? I'll help." he relented, shaken and a little afraid.

"Good," said the Dragon "and for this service I hereby appoint you as secret mapmaker to the king and wizards assistant. Do you accept this post young Tom?"

"Yes, yes your majesty and you will restore my armies?" said Tom, sitting up strait and bowing his head slightly. "Of course," said Dolphis's apparition with gentle authority.

"But only when you have completed this quest, with my trusted young wizard Alex." The digital Dolphis paused and added. "Do this well and I will reward you handsomely." Tom sat up as the Dragon disappeared from the screen. Still a little shaken he turned round and looked at Alex with a questioned look on his face. Alex just smiled and shrugged his shoulders trying not to show that he was also stunned, impressed and amazed all at the same time.

So I am Dolphis's trusted wizard he thought to himself, "that's right," whispered Dolphis in his ear to his surprise. Alex felt as if he had just grown six inches and was as proud as proud could be.

"O.K. Alex," Tom said swinging round in his chair as his computer screen went back to normal. "What do you want me to do?"

"Thanks Tom." and he went on to explain about the trip to Wales with grandad tomorrow and that they needed to find a particular spot in the mountains.

"Can you pull up all the weather data for the last few days and I want everything, every detail, and then can you fax it to grandad?"

"Consider it done bruv, --err wiz' I mean. Now, if I ask you why you and grandad have to find this spot your not gon'na tell me are you."

"If I did I'd have to pluck your heart out and feed it to the dogs," said Alex jokingly like an old pirate captain. "What's grandad up to now its buried treasure isn't it?" said Tom excitedly. Alex smiled, "Tom just know for now it's a good thing, OK."

They both laughed and slapped hands together. "I have to try and get Mia to help us yet," said Alex. "Oooh best of luck then, rather you than me, I'll see you later," said Tom turning back to his keyboard.

"Thanks big bruv." said Alex as he spun on his heels and strode out, Mia was his next target, but he had to find her first.

Pausing on the landing, He whispered to Dolphis, "how on earth did you do that?"

"I told you I could do a little magic," Dolphis said with a big grin on his face.

"Yea but that was incredible," said Alex.

Dolphis still grinning spoke "Yes, I can manipulate electrical things quite well and if I concentrate I can hear what you are thinking sometimes."

"Cool," Alex said in his inevitable understated way. "Now where on earth is Mia?"

Alex now knew that even with Dolphis sitting on his shoulder no one could see him there. So happy with that fact he peered round Mia's bedroom door after a cursory tap, tap. "Mia," he said timidly, but there was no reply. Oh well, he thought, I'll go and ask Mum if she has seen her. He trotted down the stairs and into the kitchen. There was Mum and just as she had promised, she had two picnic baskets on the table making sandwiches and wrapping things up, singing quietly to herself, as Mums often do.

"Mum, have you seen Mia?"

She looked up and said, "oh she's on the lounger in the garden dear."

"Tom's coming with us by the way," said Alex, and gave the thumbs to Mum grinning as he past her on his way outside. "Well done," she replied, and promptly carried on singing.

Alex stepped outside the back door and there sure enough was his sister on the far side of the lawn. Sixteen going on twenty one, she was lying on the lounger in her yellow bikini, smothered in suntan oil wearing a sun hat and sun glasses. Urke! (Girls) thought Alex as he wandered apprehensively over.

Mia was quite pretty with long dark hair and dark eyes but battling with that frustrating transitional period between young girl and young woman. Alex would of course understand this later in life. But for now girls in general were a total mystery to Alex.

"Mia, can I talk to you?" He said waiting for the standard reply of, -go away pest-. Instead her mobile phone rang with the tone of the latest boy band hit song. It was instantly answered with, "Hi Fiona, -- fine, ---yes, ---no, ---really, ---no, ---mmm, ---really, ---oh he didn't." Mia held out her left arm and hand gestured to Alex.

Go away----- just like an Egyptian Queen dismissing her servants. She continued with. "I know, ---mmm," ---. Alex was just about to walk away, when she pulled the phone from her ear looked at the screen in horror and almost screamed. "Oh God I've lost the signal." as if it was the end of the world. But there was worse to come, a message flashed onto the screen and she read it aloud. "Warning-your-sim-card-will-loose-all-its-memory-if-this-fault-is-not-rectifyed-in-one-minute." "Oh my God what do I do? My friends, my contacts, this can't be happening." She fumbled with the keys and was turning into a gibbering wreck. "Alex, can you remember what to do? Help me."

"Now's your chance," Dolphis whispered in his ear. "Just pretend you know what you are doing."

"Give it to me Mia"; Alex said, "I'll fix it on one condition."

"Anything, anything," she said desperately.

"Come to grandads tomorrow with us and help me with a little task."

"Yes, yes, yes anything," she said waving her arms about, "just fix it, please."

Alex confidently pressed a few buttons, paused, and pressed a few more giving the last press a dramatic double hit.

Flipping the lid shut as the final finale, he casually handed the phone back to his sister as it rang and said, still hanging on to it. "Now you won't forget about tomorrow will you?" Mia shook her head in stunned disbelief, mouth slightly open and eyeliner running down her cheeks. "You had better answer that," said Alex grinning as he let go of the phone swung round and started to walk away. "You're a darling," she shouted after him as she flicked the phone open and transformed back into sister mode. "Hello Fiona? You won't believe what just happened, yes--- mmm"----.

As he crossed the patio towards the kitchen door, Alex punched the air and shouted "Yesssssss, thanks Dolphis that was good fun and all in a good cause eh."

"Yes, and thank you Alex. I am hungry, how about you?"

"Yes," said Alex, "but I don't just fancy chewing on a few lumps of coal." They both laughed as they re entered the back door, Dolphis duly disappearing.

"Alex there you are, that sandwich over there is for you."

"Thanks Mum I'm famished can I take it up to my bedroom?"

"Oh go on then, but don't make a mess."

"Thanks," Alex shouted, as he ran up the stairs with an invisible Dolphis and the plate of sandwiches in his hand.

They both sat on the bed and made themselves comfortable. Alex opened up Dolphis's tin and gave him a chunk of charcoal and they both tucked in to their respective meals. Pausing a couple of times to chuckle at each other, both of them where very pleased indeed with the achievements of the day.

With the last sandwich in his hand Alex leapt off the bed and said, "Come on Dolphis I'll show you my car chase game."

Alex settled into the seat and switched on his PC, Dolphis was still chewing the last remnants of his charcoal on the bed, finishing with his usual small burp and little puff of smoke. "Ah that's better; I'll be with you in a moment."

"Come on hurry up," said Alex impatiently. Dolphis then stood up on his hind legs squatted and sprang a leap like a squirrel. His little wings unfolded to almost twice their size, and caught the air as he glided towards Alex's shoulder. Alex totally unaware of the incoming swung round in his chair, opened his mouth to say Dolphis, but Dolff- - was as far as he got. The little dragon tried to swerve in the air but it was too late.

Only just missing Alex's top teeth and folding his wings a tight as he could, Dolphis crashed into the remains of Alex's half chewed sandwich in his open mouth which wasn't very pleasant but at least it was a soft landing. Dolphis's tail was left dangling from Alex's lips like a wiggling worm. "Dol-ph-lif," Alex said. He was just about to eject the tangled mass from his mouth, when to his horror and at that very split second, Mum came through the door with a glass of milk in her hand.

Alex like a flash even though his eyes where starting to bulge poked the tail into his mouth and pretended to chew.

"I thought I would bring you up a nice glass of---," Mum stopped abruptly and stared at his bulging face. "Let me out then," very faintly emanated from somewhere.

Alex trying to smile rocked his head from side to side and made sort of funny sort of uubb uubb noises at the back of his throat to hide Dolphis's pleas. Mum was not impressed!

"Alex how many times have I told you not to put so much into your mouth?" she said sternly. "You'll choke," she added.

Alex spun round and spat the contents into his hands, then jumped off the chair and put it all unceremoniously into the waste bin, Dolphis and all.

"Sorry Mum," Alex said hanging his head.

"Right young man! I think it's time you got yourself ready for bed," she said firmly.

"Oh but Mum." Alex wined.

"No you have a busy day tomorrow and you will need all your sleep," said Mum.

"Can I just have one more game on my play station, please, go on please?" he pleaded. "Just one then," she said, as she put the glass of milk on the bedside table. "But then you must get ready for bed. OK."

"Alright Mum thanks," Alex said relieved.

"I'll be up to tuck you in later," Mum said as she disappeared through the door.

"Love you mum!" he shouted as he bounded towards the waste bin with a very worried look on his face. "Dolphis! Dolphis! Are you all right?"

He looked down to see his friend covered in bits of sandwich trying to free himself from the gooey mess. "Let me help you," said Alex concerned.

"Purthrat, erg," Dolphis spat several times as Alex reached into the bin and gingerly picked him out. "That was a close one," said Dolphis with a gooey smile.

"Come on I'll get you cleaned up in the bathroom sink," said Alex picking off a particularly sticky lump of sandwich from the top of Dolphis's head while he walked to the bathroom.

Alex ran the taps in the bathroom sink until the temperature was just right, put the plug in, and filled the sink with just a few centimetres of hot water. Dolphis checked the temperature with his tail and slid down into the steaming water.

"Oow ah owww that's good," said Dolphis as Alex handed him an old toothbrush.

"Scrub yourself down with that," he laughed. Alex watched as Dolphis did his best and seemed to be quite enjoying himself. "We dragons do bath you know, but only once or twice a year," he said laughing.

Alex noticed a few shiny patches appearing and while the water had removed all the gloopy bits it was turning a little black. "Here, give me that brush a minute," said Alex.

Alex started to brush Dolphis's scaly back gently, adding just a little shampoo.

Before long Dolphis, who by this time was almost purring like a cat with enjoyment, had started to turn from a greeny black to the shiniest gold you could imagine.

His fine scales reflecting the light like a butterfly, even his wings where gold.

"Wow! Dolphis, your beautiful." said Alex slowly.

"Why thank you kind sir," he said with a cheeky grin and bowing like a prince.

"Come on lets get you dried off," Alex said, reaching for the towel.

Dolphis now cleaned and sparkling was carried back into the bedroom and placed on Alex's pillow. Alex stood back and said, "It's a total transformation I can't believe it."

Dolphis looked at Alex and spoke quite seriously. "This is why we were hunted and killed by you humans you know, it's our bio-metallic skin you see. The outer surface is solid gold and our bones are made of black gold the rarest, hardest gold there is."

"I'm sorry I do understand now Dolphis, we human beings are really selfish and cruel sometimes, and I promise to help you and your kin in any way I can, always."

Alex picked Dolphis up with both hands and lifted him up to his face.

"Dolphis you are my extraordinary friend and I will not let you down."

Dolphis smiled, "that go's for me too, my friend."

A few silent moments past then Alex cleared his throat and said smartly. "Dolphis lets have some fun before bedtime, I'll quickly get ready for bed and we'll have a go at my car chase game."

"Good idea my friend," said Dolphis smiling again.

Alex picked up the glass of milk and drank it down in one, "Greeeeeeeeeaaaaaaat" Said Alex in one long burp.

They both laughed and played as good friends do, Dolphis showing Alex how he could control the computer by just touching and they had a lot of fun, but they both tired quickly.

They decided it was time for bed. Alex got ready, and Dolphis climbed back into his matchbox home. "See you tomorrow," Alex said yawning, and then climbed into bed. Within minutes the pair where fast asleep. Mum just as she had promised came up later on and tucked Alex in. It was going to be a hell of a day tomorrow.

Chapter 5.

The Bad Guys.

Alex woke to the sound of his Mum's voice. "Come on Alex its Six thirty, breakfast in twenty minutes, we will want to be off by seven thirty at the latest."

Alex Mumbled as he turned over, he had been dreaming about car chases, dragons and strangely, coal sandwiches. He opened his eyes, as Mum shook his shoulder gently.

"I would get to the bathroom before your sister," she said, as she disappeared through the door. Alex sat up in bed and rubbed his eyes, climbing out of bed he went over to the matchbox balancing on the transformer. He picked it up and slid the draw open, there was Dolphis curled up and still asleep. "Morning Dolphis," Alex said excitedly. Dolphis stirred, yawned and looked up at Alex. "Today's the day, little friend," said Alex, and he carried him over to the window were they where both greeted by a lovely sunny day. "Enjoy the view Dolphis I'm going to get washed and dressed, be back in a minute. Oh and here's your breakfast." Alex opened the little tin, which he had replenished curtsey of the barbecue, and carefully picked out a nice chunk of charcoal. "Thanks," said Dolphis, as Alex rushed out to the bathroom.

Dolphis was contently chewing on his breakfast looking through the bedroom window, when he noticed a big black van with blacked out windows parked on the quiet country road to the right of the house just underneath some trees. Just then the passenger door opened and an oriental looking man got out, went round the back of the van, and re-entered through the back doors.

Dolphis shivered and instinctively knew this was trouble and backed away from the window. A cold chill went through his little body, where these the men his family had always warned him about, Dragon hunters?

He cowered down and crawled back into the matchbox, if they had Dragon detector devices, the silver aluminium foil would perhaps shield him at least.

Dolphis wasn't afraid of much but he knew that if these men got hold of him, he would never see his family again.

Where was Alex? He had been a long time, thought Dolphis nervously.

Eventually Alex come sauntering back in. "Dolphis I've just been talking to Tom and all the info was sent to grandad last night and also Toms printed off some maps for us."

"Great Alex, but I think we may have another problem," still keeping his head low in the matchbox. Dolphis pointed to the black van parked out on the verge. Alex kneeled on the bed to look out the window.

"Oh that's Mr. Chang's Dodge," Alex said. "He's the gardener from the big estate just up the road, mmmm owned by a pop star or famous actor I think. I've only ever seen him once, a big fat guy Yes, Mr. Chang and his brother work for him. I've often seen them in the village post office, sending parcels back to china."

Alex stopped abruptly and looked at his friend. "What sort of trouble Dolphis?"

"My instinct tells me they are dragon hunters and they will stop at nothing," said Dolphis. "Let me explain. It all goes back to a secret Chinese Dragon cult, hundreds of years ago. They thought that owning a dragon gave them special powers. And even now some people still believe this, and of course this makes us almost priceless. Not just for the gold in my body but for the status of owning such a rare thing. Of course it is true that an object made from the gold in my skin brings good luck, but it only works if it is freely given." Dolphis looked quite sad and slunk back even further into his matchbox.

"Look Dolphis don't worry, you have us to help you now, and if these men are what you say, we will find a way to stop them," he said confidently. "I'll get Mia to phone grandad he will know what to do."

Alex quickly dressed, crossed the landing and knocked on Mia's door saying, "It's Alex, can I borrow your mobile, to phone Grandad?" The door opened a few inches and the phone appeared already ringing Grandads number. Grandad's voice answered almost instantly. "Hello, hello, who's that?" Alex still in shock at Mia's unselfish act hesitated then put the phone to his ear. "Oh, oh, grandad we have a slight problem."

"What is it young Alex what's up?"

Alex went on to describe as fast as he could all the events leading up to this moment in time and especially Dolphis's concerns about Mr. Chang and his brother.

The phone went almost quiet for a few moments, and Alex could hear grandad thinking out loud. "Mmmm mm yes mmmm. OK Alex! I think Dolphis himself may have the answer to this one, can you ask him how close he needs to be to an electrical device to access it?"

"I'll hold the phone close to Dolphis; you can both talk to each other then."

"Good idea Alex"grandad said, and a conversation was soon going on between the two of them. Dolphis started to smile. "Right you are," said Dolphis and nodded to Alex.

Alex put the phone back to his ear. "Granddad," said Alex.

"Now my boy, Dolphis will explain it all to you and you be careful young man."

"OK grandad, see you later, by." Alex flipped the phone shut and delivered it back to Mia who was just coming out of her bedroom. "Thank you." said Alex.

Mia just smiled and said, "Don't forget breakfast in fifteen minutes."

Alex rushed back to Dolphis. "Now what's the plan Dolphis?"

"Well, grandad tells me that most modern cars have an ECU or electronic control unit. This controls all sorts of things on a vehicle and if you can get me close enough to touch the van, I should be able to alter a few things to make life interesting for Mr. Chang and his brother."

"Right I'll get Tom to set up a kind of diversion or something after breakfast, let's go and talk to him now." Alex slipped Dolphis and the matchbox into his pocket and found Tom in his bedroom just turning off his computer. "Tom I need your help again." said Alex.

"I am yours to command little Wiz." he smiled.

Alex went on to explain how He thought Mr. Changs van would be a danger to grandads secret mission if they followed them. Without going into to much detail, Alex said he thought they were sort of spies, and if Tom could create a diversion he would somehow sabotage the van. "Tom what do you think?"

"You can then leave the rest to me little brother I have an idea already, we'll meet after breakfast by the front door, but we won't have much time though." said Tom. The two brothers smiled slapped hands together and went down to breakfast.

All the family were now busily tucking in to a hearty breakfast, Mum had already finished hers and was starting to clear things away.

"You children can come with me in the estate car, we will follow dad in the MG to grandads." "Yes Mum." Was the reply in almost complete unison from the three children.

Dad looked at Mum and almost choked on his toast, Mum stood in silence for a few moments waiting for the usual infighting, but the children just carried on eating there breakfast.

"OK then" Mum said sort of stunned. "Mia, you can help me put the picnic stuff in the estate, and you boys can make sure Woody's food and water is topped up and in the car."

"OK Mum." Another reply in complete unison. Dad shrugged his shoulders and looked at Mum who was still taken aback by this unusual behaviour, they both smiled in a surprised sort of way and carried on with what ever they where doing.

A few minutes later dad had finished his toast, got up from the table and said, "I'll get old no 8 out, check her over, and ready for the road." "OK darling we'll all be ready in twenty minutes." said Mum.

Breakfast things cleared away and all tasks completed, Tom and Alex rushed down to the old garden shed, where Tom kept his secret arsenal of home made weapons.

Bows and arrows, sling shots, and a catapult, Tom picked up the catapult and looked at Alex, they both smiled, this was the chosen weapon for today's task. They regrouped by the front door as planned.

Tom laid out his plan to Alex as they discussed details.

"OK Alex you need to get to the front of the van to do what ever magic you have to do. I'll fire a stone at the back window of the van when a car goes by from behind that tree. If I get it right the glass will just shatter. They will come out to have a look, by this time I will be by the back of the van laying on the ground moaning and groaning as if I have been hurt, and I might just get a peek inside the back too." "Brilliant" said Alex. "Let's go."

They both slipped instantly into commando mode, luckily there where plenty of shrubs and trees to give them both cover as they took up positions ready for the assault. Tom had already selected a couple of spiky looking flints as his missiles and got into position.

Alex whispered to Dolphis as they hid just a few feet from the van. "Ready for action my little friend?"

"Yes." said Dolphis's muffled voice. " And don't open my box until you are certain we are OK as soon as you open it they will be able to detect me."

"No problemo." said Alex and they settled down to wait for a car to come by.

Minutes past like hours, when suddenly the whoosh of tyres on the road and the faint sound of an engine could be heard coming along the quiet country lane. The car had to be coming towards the back of the van for the plan to work, and luckily it was. Whoosh it went by, dust and leaves billowing in its wake. And with a crack! The back window shattered. Tom was in position within a few seconds, writhing and moaning behind the van. Both front doors opened and Mr. Chang and his brother jumped out both waiving fists and probably shouting rude words in Chinese at the car as it sped off into the distance.

Tom moaned loudly and the two brothers turned to investigate. Heading round the back of the van they found Tom lying on the ground. Mr. Chang said. "We no see you, where you come from?" Tom moaned a bit more, and Alex saw his chance, he jumped out from his hiding place and crouched in front of the car. He pulled the matchbox from his pocket and slid it open. Dolphis stood up and touched the metalwork with his tiny claws, and went into deep concentration.

The Chang brothers where now bending over Tom gesturing and arguing with each other in Chinese. After a while, Tom still moaning was helped to his feet and was being dusted off by the two brothers. "Where it hurt, you OK yes?" Mr. Chang said more worried about some huge insurance claim than Tom's well-being.

Tom could now see inside the van through the broken back window. He took a mental note of the strange huge oriental clock like instrument strapped to side of the van. It had two large dials each with a single ornately decorated single hand. Both of which where swinging wildly round and pointing to strange caricatures instead of numbers. This in turn triggering little trap doors that slid open along the bottom of the what looked like a very ancient carved wooden case. The hands suddenly stopped and pointed at each other and it looked like just one more trap door was left to open. Tom pretended to stagger a little and as the brothers reached forward to steady him, he saw Alex slip away back into the bushes. Tom took one last glance at the strange clock, the hands had dropped and all the little trap doors had closed. His job was done.

Tom pretended to come back to his senses. "Where am I?" he said as he rubbed his head. "You plenty fine now." said Mr. Chang.

Just then dad turned up to see what all the commotion was about. "What's happened here then Tom? Hello Mr. Chang."

Mr. Chang and his brother bowed there heads slightly as they turned round.

Tom piped up immediately, "I tripped and fell over behind Mr. Changs van, they where just helping me up."

"Are you OK Tom?" dad said as Tom came over towards him. Dad examined his head and looked him over.

"Number one son plenty good no damage." said Mr. Chang with a toothy grin, his brother nodding in agreement.

"Well you look OK to me." said dad. "What where you doing here Mr. Chang, I see you have a broken window?"

"We look for rare mushroom in woods, very tasty, mad fast car go by, break window. Number one son fall over, all ok now, we go soon," said Mr. Chang as he edged his way back to the front of the van. The brothers bowed again pretending to be as polite as possible and jumped back into the van.

Dad and Tom turned and started to walk back up the drive. "Are you sure you are OK Tom?" said dad, as he put his arm round him.

"Yes I'm fine dad honestly."

"Go on then run up to house and change those shorts, they are filthy." "And don't be long, we are off soon" dad shouted as Tom sped off to the house.

Alex was waiting on the landing as Tom raced up the stairs. "You were brilliant Tom." Alex said excitedly.

"Did you do your magic Ok?" Said Tom.

"We will see-- if they try and follow us." said Alex.

Tom went on to describe the strange clock like device he saw in the back of the van. "I'll draw a picture of it for you when we get to grandads."

"OK" said Alex, who was thinking to himself, it looks like Dolphis, was right.

"I reckon they are spies all right Tom, we will have to be on our guard."

Alex wanted to share his secret with his brother there and then, but Tom seemed happy to go along with his plans for now. Tom had showed his mettle and it was a good feeling for both the brothers to be united in this task. "All for one, one for all, eh little wiz" said Tom out of the blue, with a huge grin on his face. Alex held out his hand for a double up down slap, and said

"I can't see Mia as a musketeer somehow." They both laughed as they busily set about getting ready for the task ahead.

"Come on you two! we are ready to go." shouted Mum up the stairs. Tom gathered up the maps, Alex checked his pocket to make sure Dolphis was there and the two brothers scampered off excitedly towards what had become a shared adventure.

Chapter 6

Heading for the Hills.

The little convoy was nearly ready to go; Mum was doing her usual fussing around checking all was present and correct. While Mia had just remembered she needed an essential item of makeup, and had gone to find it. Meanwhile dad walked up to the open back door window of the estate car where Tom and Alex where seated. "Tom do you want to ride with me today, if that's OK with Mum?"

"Fine with me" she smiled "just make sure you put your seat belt on."

"Thanks dad I'd like that" and he climbed out of his seat. "See you later Alex."

Dad patted Alex on the head through the window, "you're still my chief mechanic old boy." "I know dad" said Alex smiling.

Mia was now getting back into her seat and rearranging things. Woody was huffing and panting in the back of the estate car. His huge tail wagged expectantly, while his tongue hung from the side of his mouth and dribbled like a wet sponge on the seat behind Alex.

"Settle down now Woody." Mum said sternly, turning round in her seat. He obeyed instantly and sat down licking his lips with a sort of doggy moan.

At last they where ready to go, dad waved his arm in the air in a circular fashion to indicate, start your engines, and they pulled out of the drive. The black van was still parked up at the front of the house and Alex kept a very close eye on it in the rear view mirror. His heart sank as he saw the van pull off the grass and start to follow them. Then almost immediately a great plume of black smoke billowed from the rear of the van and it lurched to halt in the middle of the road.

He could just make out two irate figures leaping out and waving there arms in the air as they sped away. Alex very relieved, chuckled to himself and whispered "it worked Dolphis."

Alex settled back in his seat and watched the trees and fields go by as the morning sun climbed ever higher in the deep blue sky.

Before long the convoy was turning off into grandad's driveway, this time taking the driveway off to the back of the house towards the old barn. The huge door was already open and grandad was strapping things to the side of Spitty outside on the courtyard.

The family all got out of the cars and stood around Spitty, even Mia said "it's lovely grandad."

"Nearly ready boys and girls, I've phoned uncle Nige and said we'll be there in a couple of hours, the hill climb is just down the road from him, so we won't have far to go to give the old girl a run up the hill." Grandad winked at Alex. "I've converted the old girl to run on a special bio fuel I've invented. She's still a bit thirsty so I'm taking a bit extra." Grandad said pointing to tanks strapped round the car.

"What's this grandad?" said Tom, leaning over the door and pointing to what looked like a miniature modern version of what he saw in the back of the black van.

Brrrrrfff brrrr grandad cleared his throat nervously, "That's my radar detector." Referring to the strange looking device. "You can't be too careful you know."

"Grandad" said Mum with a concerned look on her face.

"Don't worry my dear I won't be doing anything silly with such a valuable cargo aboard." he said with a reassuring smile and gesturing at the children.

"Don't worry Mum." said Mia, "I'll keep on eye on them." "Mmmm."said Mum shaking her head.

All this time Dolphis had been fast asleep in Alex's pocket, but had now woken up and wriggled out of his box and climbed onto Alex's shoulder, in invisible mode of course.

Mum said to dad. "I am just going to take woody for a quick 5 minute run in the woods, coming dear?" Dad whistled several times and said, "Come on boy." and the three of them headed off through the woods.

Granddad then gathered the children around him, "Now boys and girls he said, you know we have a little bit of a task to perform?" yes, they all nodded in unison. This is really Alex's mission and we all under his command so to speak. He gathered Alex in front of him, over to you young man."

"Well." Alex started off coyly, "All this is for a friend of mine, and he needs to get back to his family." "What friend?" said Mia, "Yes." piped in Tom.

"Well," Alex started again, but this time was interrupted by Dolphis.

"It's OK said a little voice; we are all in this together, Tom and Mia you need to know the truth." Tom was totally lost for words as he looked around to try and see where the little voice had come from. Mia tapped her phone several times and was mystified. Dolphis then appeared on Alex's shoulder in all his glory. There was silence for a few seconds. "Woohh the King of the West." said Tom.

"Oh what a sweet little thing" Mia said smiling, quite unfazed. "Can I stroke him?" Dolphis sort of blushed in his own dragon way. "First, I will tell you quickly the story of how I came to be here and how Alex, Grandad, and of course now you two sort of volunteered to help me get back home.

Over the next few minutes Grandad Alex and Dolphis laid out the story and the plan to Mia and Tom, who could hardly take their eyes of the little dragon.

"Dragon hunter's eh." said Tom, we'll show them. "A bit like the three Musketeers." said Mia? Tom and Alex looked at each other and laughed. A little group hug followed.

Grandad then stood back clapped his hands together, "Right then crew lets get organised before the others get back, Tom you are in the front with me, and you can operate this device I savaged from a Chinese junk when I was in Hong Kong, never did know what it was until now," he laughed. "Alex and Dolphis you two are in charge of maps etc, all the maps we will need I hope, are in these Jenks type roller map holders, you will see how they work it is quite simple. Mia In the back, the box in front of your seat, holds four communication devices, your job is to collate all information and keep us all in touch.

Dolphis this small box in the middle is a Faraday cage so you can see out but not be detected if we spot any danger. Don't worry little chap it opens from the inside or outside. You can get in or out when ever you fancy," said grandad, looking reassuringly at Dolphis. Ok everybody, while you take up your positions I have one more thing to get from the house. Granddad sauntered off while the children and Dolphis all climbed into their seats and set about checking things out like seasoned troops.

Meanwhile Mum and dad had returned and were walking up to the children seated in Spitty. "Make way for Woody you lot" said dad, "I see grandad has fixed a mat to the centre of the rear seat for him, so he doesn't slide around, good," he said opening the door.

Woody jumped in and dutifully took his position between Mia and Alex.

Mum was checking that the picnic baskets were strapped on properly on both cars, when grandad came back carrying six army surplus thermos flasks. "Ginger beer for all" he said, grinning from ear to ear. He placed them in a leather case on the floor between the back seats. "There you go my beauties; OK lets get going then everybody.

Grandad pulled a leaver by the side of the barn door and the huge door clanked and whirred as it swung shut. "I'll take the lead then" he said as he climbed into his seat and put on an old flying helmet. "Have you locked up?" said Mum loudly to grandad, "yes my sentries are on guard" he said, referring to two stone gargoyles at the front and back doors. Mum smiled and shook her head, "I'm sure he's bonkers" she said to dad as she got back into old no 8.

All now ready for the off the whole family were quite excited as they waited for grandad to start up Spitty. He primed the engine set the ignition and with a shout of "chocks away" pressed the starter button. A shrill sound like a high speed electric drill filled the air as the mighty engine turned over, cough,spit,cough,cough,pat,pat, PAROOM,

BAROOM,BAROOM,BAROOMMMM, Spitty's engine did indeed sound like a second word war spitfire starting up, they all held their ears as Mia Shouted over the roar "GRANDAD!" Grandad laughed as he operated a leaver on the dashboard and the exhaust note quietened to a wonderful off beat thobbity throb, throbbity throb, throbbity throb. All ready to go, said grandad as he checked over Spittys instruments and gave the thumbs up to Brian, Spitty pulled away as gentle as a kitten followed by Mum and dad and the classic convoy slid out on to the quiet country roads and headed for the Welsh hills.

Settling into a steady pace in the morning sunshine, they all enjoyed the warm morning air drifting over them as they watched the glorious countryside go by. Time went by quite quickly while Tom, Alex and Mia were studying their various instruments.

Grandad had written a little book of instructions for each device and these were hanging on a piece of string attached to each instrument.

For some reason Woody paid absolutely no attention to Dolphis apart from the odd look and occasional sniff and was quite happy to let him snuggle in his fur. In fact even the odd dribble from Woody's tongue did not detract from this new and unusual friendship.

Alex although enjoying the journey was still keeping a wary eye open for any sign of the black van. Often turning around and checking while giving a cheery wave to Mum and dad, following up the rear in old no 8.

Tom was reading his book of instructions for the second time, carefully pressing the strange shaped buttons and observing the way the hands in the dials reacted.

Then all of a sudden the dials swung together and pointed to each other as if by some strange magnetic attraction. The trap doors along the bottom started to open one by one, revealing Chinese caricatures as they went. "Look at this" Tom shouted, Alex leaned forward and looked over his shoulder. Tom thumbed through the little book as each caricature was revealed. Tom shouted out the meaning of each as he found them in his book. "Dragon,-------Life-force,--------Southeast,--------Zero,--------Zero.

Grandad still concentrating on the road ahead, said "Alex look at the compass by your maps, which way is southeast?" "OK grandad" it's, it's, right behind us." Right Dolphis old chap, can you jump into your Faraday cage.

Dolphis did as he was asked and closed the door behind him. Instantly the dials on the old box started to swing round and each trap door shut in reverse order.

"Just as I thought he said, that old box must pick up Dolphis's electro magnetic signal, let's hope our Chinese friends haven't got a fix on us yet.

Dolphis, can you stay in the cage for a little while longer? I reckon we have about 30 minutes before we get to Uncle Nigel's."

"I'm fine in here and it's out of the draught and quite warm in here" was the cheery reply from Dolphis.

Dolphis could smell the change in the air as the bends in the road got tighter; the convoy was starting to climb the mountain roads now, and while grandad swung the old Bentley round changing up and down through the gears, he would talk gently to the old car. "Come on old girl, an easy right hander a touch of brake and on with the throttle, ha ha lovely old thing" and he patted the dashboard. Alex could see back into the valley below as they swooped effortlessly round the hairpins. There was no sign of a black van, just dad and Mum a few hundred yards behind them. Dolphis had now snuggled back up with woody in the back seat and as they rounded the next corner a beautiful stretch of wide strait road opened up before them with nothing on it as far as the eye could see. Grandad looked at Tom and Alex, and they all smiled at once. Mia piped up "Grandad NO!" "Just going to check if the supercharger is working ok, what did you say my dear" he said with wicked smile on his face. Hang on boys and girls. Grandad moved a lever on the dash to full boost, flicked the exhaust lever open and with the sound of a low flying aircraft the old Bentley shot forward like a formula one car. Grandad's eyes narrowed with intense concentration as the speed rose rapidly. Mia let out a little scream, but was actually enjoying the sensation, for those few seconds it felt like Spitty was almost flying and then just as quickly grandad eased off the throttle and shut the levers down. As they coasted back down to the normal speed, every one was quite exhilarated even Mia, who tried not to show it. Alex looked round but Mum and dad were no where to be seen, yet there was a car coming up behind them. Oh no it had a blue flashing light, "grandad, grandad" shouted Alex, "it's a police car."

"I can see it in my mirror old chap, better pull over in this lay-by then." Grandad slowed down and swung into the lay-by, pulled on the outside handbrake and slumped back in his seat looking quite depressed. The police car had now stopped behind them; still with its lights flashing and the two officers alighted. They put there caps on and walked up to the old Bentley. The officer on grandad's side pushed his cap back on his head and scratched his forehead all the while looking at the car from front to back. "Morning officer lovely day" said grandad. The other younger officer was at the back punching in details on a hand held computer thing, and had obviously only just left school. Mia smiled at the young man, pulled out her compact and started to adjust her hair and makeup, and he smiled back.

"Morning Sir," said the officer beside grandad, "can I see your driving licence please?" Grandad pulled it from his pocket and handed it to him.

"Well Sir it doesn't say Jenson Button here, do you know what speed you where doing?" There was a pause "just a little over the limit was I?"

"A little, a little, the officer exclaimed, my detector was off the dial before it all went dead, some sort of magnetic interference I guess, you are very lucky indeed sir and if I catch you speeding like that on a public road again I'll throw the book at you." The officer relaxed and nodded towards Spitty, "she's a beauty though sir, off to the hill climb then are we?"

Mum and dad had now pulled in behind them; dad got out and walked over to the officer. "Every thing all right officer?" "Yes, just telling Jensen here to watch his speed, there's a lot of sheep wandering about these parts, wouldn't want you to have an accident now would we," and he handed grandad back his licence. Grandad coughed and spluttered a little, cleared his throat and said, "Thank you very much officer I'll certainly be careful." "You do that sir and by the way my brother's racing on the hill today in Beastie 2, rear engine job you know. So I might even see you later, good day sir."

The officer turned to walk back to the patrol car, come on Romeo" and he grabbed the young officers arm that had been transfixed by Mia. They walked back and got into the patrol car, turned the flashing lights off and within a minute where speeding back to their hiding place up the road.

Dad gave grandad a sideways look, and said "come on then let's get going, only a few more miles to go."

Almost immediately they where back on the road and it wasn't long before the sign to the village where Uncle Nigel lived came into view, turning off the main road and round a few more hilly bends, they were almost there. Passing stone cottages and a pub with slate tiled roofs, another little lane led off to the old farmhouse that grandads best friend had made his home. Grandad pressed the klaxon horn on Spitty and a gritty sounding, OOH-AAAH, echoed loudly around the valley and announced their arrival.

As soon as the two cars pulled up in the courtyard of Nigel's old farmhouse, the front door flung open and the whole family emerged one by one, Uncle Nigel limping slightly on his gammy leg, caused by a motorcycle accident many years ago. Everyone was out of their cars by now and Alex had carefully slipped Dolphis into the matchbox and back into his pocket.

Mum was kissing and cuddling everyone in turn and there must have been at least four generations of Uncle Nigel's family out there to greet them all.

Grandad was already reminiscing with his old friend Nigel, bonnet up on Spitty, laughing and joking like a pair of schoolboys as they walked round the car.

Amidst excited laughter and chatter, a steady procession of what every body felt was their extended family reacquainted themselves with each other. Husbands, wives and children it was indeed a happy reunion. Alex spotted James, Lee's eldest son, standing between Lee and his Dad. Lee was Uncle Nigel's son and a good friend of his dad, both men where eagerly chatting and examining old no 8 as Alex sauntered over to James who was about the same age as him. "Hi'ya James, have you still got Ferociously Fast, for your PS2?"

James grinned "hi Alex, better than that I have FF2! Got it for my birthday last week." "Well cool" Said Alex. "Do you want to have a go?" said James. "Wicked" exclaimed Alex. "Dad" both boys said in unison and then giggled.

"Go in then, half an hour max" said Lee, and they nodded in agreement. The two boys shot off like rifle bullets as dad and Lee got deeper into conversation about camshafts, valves and other things mechanical.

Just about the same time Nigel's wife Kathleen came outside carrying a huge tray of butterscotch tarts. Now Kathleen who never revealed her age but never looked more than 45, was as far as the family concerned and

Tom particularly, the best cook in the world. Tom's mouth watered at the prospect of Auntie Kathleen's butterscotch tart, and he raced over to be the first in line. A big pot of tea was already on the picnic table outside as Mum emerged from the house with a big tray of squash and lemonade. Mia with Hannah who was another granddaughter of Nigel and Kathleen, followed behind Mum carrying glass's and cups for the various beverages.

Although still quite early in the morning every one felt in a sort of carnival mood as the children played in the big courtyard laughing and running in between the groups of adults followed by woody doing his best to join in the activity, wagging his tail ten to the dozen.

Nigel and Grandad then stood up in Spitty; Nigel spoke up raising his voice so every one could hear. "Right every body, those that are coming we leave in about 20 minutes, we have to get to Westfarland hill to qualify for the race this afternoon."

Chapter 7.

Dolphis gets closer to home.

Meanwhile over in the cottage where James lived Alex had finished his turn on the PS2, thanking James he said "see you later at the hill climb maybe" waving goodbye he made his way outside and climbed the small hillock behind the row of cottages opposite the old farmhouse. Dolphis was looking out of his pocket as they reached the top of the hill. Looking down into the valley they both had a good view. Alex still wary of any danger scoured the countryside for any sign of a black van or anything that might be trouble.

Satisfied the coast was clear he reached into his pocket and Dolphis climbed onto his hand. Holding him gently between his clasped hands, Alex said "Not long now my little friend if all goes well, I am going to miss you." "And I you" Dolphis said sadly.

"Will you be allowed to visit me sometimes" said Alex. "Only if you're allowed to come and visit me" said Dophis grinning.

They both cheered up a little. "I suppose we ought to be getting back" said Alex. He turned and raced back down the hill putting Dolphis back in his pocket as he ran. "Come on lets see what grandad's plan is." Dolphis was being tumbled around in Alex's pocket as he jogged towards Spitty. "Steady on" said a muffled voice from Alex's pocket, "ooh sorry" said Alex as he slowed to a walking pace. "That's ok said Dolphis" spitting out lumps of fluff. "Any chance of some ginger beer?" "You don't give up do you" chuckled Alex, "alright I'll ask grandad."

The convoy had started to assemble with the addition of Nigel's Morgan aero 3 wheeler and Lee's methanol burning V twin special motorcycle, which was on a trailer hitched behind his car.

Grandad was topping up the fuel tank on Spitty as Alex tapped him on the back.

"Grandad" "yes Alex" said grandad turning his head. "Dophis would like some ginger beer" "Right you are, pop over to that empty barn over there, I'll be with you in a minute." "OK," said Alex and walked over to the barn door which was just ajar and slipped inside. Coming in from the bright sunshine outside it was very dark inside the old barn. Grandad followed through the door a few minutes later. By now Alex's eyes were getting used to the darkness, and he could just make out a small glass bottle and a thimble that grandad was carrying.

Dolphis jumped from Alex's pocket onto an old box in the middle of the floor. Rubbing his little clawed hands together and sitting up on his hind legs, he looked up and smiled obviously looking forward too his treat. Grandad carefully poured out half a thimble full of his famous ginger beer and handed it to Dolphis. "Try that young Dolphis! It'll put hairs on your chest," laughed grandad.

Dolphis tipped up the cup and poured it down his throat in one gulp. "Ahhhh --hic" and two rings of blue smoke popped from his nostrils. "Excellent he said, now stand back and watch this." Dolphis arched his back and gripped the box with his claws, took a deep breath and started to blow, instantly a blue flame erupted like the afterburner of a miniature jet engine. The force was so powerful the box started to move across the floor. Grandad and Alex stepped back in amazement and for a few seconds after Dolphis's demonstration they where dumbfounded. Finally they all drew breath and Dolphis looked up and said with a big smile on his face, "that was a burp and a half eh boys? Alex and Grandad nodded simultaneously still stunned.

"By George I've never seen anything like it" stuttered grandad. "Mega cool" said Alex.

"Ok you guys, we have to get back on the road" said grandad, coming back to his senses adding. "And you Dolphis, you are indeed an extraordinary Dragon."

"Thank you kind sir, you're not so bad yourself" said Dolphis. Grandad smiled as Alex bent down to pick Dolphis up and said most concerned "are you ok, not burnt or any thing?" "I am absolutely fine" said Dolphis smiling and feeling very pleased with himself.

"Come on before they wonder what we are doing chaps" said Grandad swinging round and heading for the door.

Grandad and Alex joined with the rest of the family milling round the courtyard readying themselves for the off. Woody had taken up position with Kathleen and somehow knew that once the cavalcade had departed a walk in the hills and a nice doggy treat was his compensation for staying behind.

The convoy was now assembled, with the addition of several more cars packed to the gunnels with Uncle Nigel's family members. Turning round and checking that every one was ready, all the engines started one by one and the signal was given by Uncle Nigel to move off.

Heading the coulomb in his old Morgan the line of splendid machinery circled the big courtyard, and every one waved to those left behind as the convoy made its way back out to the main road.

Westfarland hill was only a few miles away so it wasn't long before the convoy joined a cavalcade of machinery heading for the event and was entering the main gate for competitors.

On joining the queues of ancient and modern vehicles being directed to the paddock by marshals and officials. Each competitor collected the necessary paperwork while being directed to their allotted spot.

Grandad leant out over his door as he spotted an old friend in a white coat directing cars. Drawing up along side him he raised his voice over the engine noise. "Hi Jim, how's the old Allard going?" "Blew the back axle in practice, so I'm a spectator today."

"Bad luck old bean, come and have a ginger beer with us later" laughed grandad.

"Will do, your crew is up there on the left" Jim pointed to several empty spaces' see you later" said Jim. Uncle Nigel was already backing his Morgan into his pit space as the old Bentley pulled into its spot.

Grandad turned off the engine and relaxed back in his seat. "Well boys and girls we are here" he said with a twinkle in his eye. Within a few minutes Mum, Dad, Lee and all had arrived and were unpacking various bits and pieces needed for the day's competition.

Grandad and the children where unstrapping and removing all surplus to requirement things off Spitty, while admiring groups of spectators walked past looking at the many varied and different machines parked in the paddock.

Grandad then gathered all the three children at the back of Spitty, Dolphis of course still in Alex's pocket. He bent down on one knee and drew the children close to him. "Ok every body I've arranged to qualify early so we can slip out for a few hours on a supposed test run in Spitty. This will be our chance to get Dolphis back to his home and Family. According to mine and Tom's research, that group of hills up there," pointing behind the children to what looked like mountains penetrating the clouds, "will be our destination."

They all looked round, Dolphis peeping out of the top of Alex's pocket. "There you are my little friend" said Alex.

Dolphis smiled a little Dragon smile "I can almost smell my home" and he drew in a deep breath through his nostrils.

"Right then children and friends," grandad said nodding towards Dolphis. "Just my racing numbers to put on and I'll give the old girl a blast up the hill."

Just then the tannoy speakers crackled into life. "Will the following competitors assemble at scrutineering for the first qualifying runs of the day, 10, 4, 26 and 17 thank you?"

"That's you grandad, 26," the children shouted excitedly. "Yep" said grandad walking round Spitty giving her a final check over. Dolphis leapt from Alex's pocket and made his way to the front passenger's seat, in invisible mode of course. Grandad had now got into Spitty and was looking in the passenger's foot well for his old crash helmet. "Can I come too" said Dolphis in his ear? "Ooh you made me jump I didn't see you there" said grandad pulling out his helmet.

The children had gathered together and were looking over the top of the door as Dolphis reappeared on the seat. "It could be dangerous you know old chap" advised Grandad. Dolphis just smiled and looked at them all, "I like going fast in Spitty," he said in an appealing sort of way. Mia piped up, "well grandad, Spitty hasn't got a mascot and Dophis is rather beautiful." "Yes" they all said.

"OK then, up on the dash behind the windscreen," grandad patted the centre of the dashboard. "But you must keep absolutely still and at least you will get a good view from up here. Right you lot, let's not waste any more time" and he buckled up and slid on his helmet. Everyone stood back as grandad got ready to start up Spitty. "Ear plugs in" he shouted, and they all gave the thumbs up sign.

The starter engaged and Spitty gave a mighty roar accompanied by a cloud of light blue smoke that smelt strangely of fish and chips.

Grandad and Dolphis pulled gently away, Spittys mighty engine throbbing effortlessly as they made there way down the slight incline towards the scrutineering bay, where two men in white coats holding clipboards were there waiting for them.

By now all the family where on their way to the start line fence, where they could get a good view of Spittys launch off the line. First to go up was a beautiful blue Bugatti. Already on the start line with the chock man stationed on the near side rear wheel to stop it rolling backwards. Blaaa, Blaaaaa, Blaaaaaaaaaaaaaaaaaa the engine revved and he shot off the line with a little smoke from the rear wheels. Blaaaaaaaaoooooohhh the Bugatti sped past on his way up the hill. The exhaust sounding like a calico sheet being torn in half, magnified a thousand times.

Grandad, Dolphis and Spitty had got through scrutineering and were now waiting behind two cars ready to go up the hill. The excitement was now growing in the whole family as the last car in front of Spitty blasted away from the line in a cloud of tyre smoke and on up the hill. Spitty and her crew were now in position, the engine coughing and spitting almost as if she was clearing her throat. The engine roared and a crescendo of sound erupted as Spitty leaped off the line. As she flew past Alex could see the glint of gold on the dashboard and grandad working hard at the wheel to keep her on his chosen line. Many spectators with hands over their ears where cheering as Spitty thundered by. Grandad and Spitty disappeared as he entered the second row of bends and reappeared a few seconds later sliding unto the tight hairpin that would take him further up the hill, the great engine roared as he disappeared again into the tree lined track and up the twisting hill towards the final mile and finishing line. They could still hear the engine crackling and popping as grandad came off the throttle and over the line in the distance.

The whole family jumped up and down with excitement as they waited for the time to be announced over the Tannoy. "One minute forty seven seconds a good qualifying run by no 26," announced the commentator. They all cheered again.

But Alex was clinging to the fence oblivious of the celebrations. Peering through to the other side of the track, he could just make out two Chinese characters he had seen before. It was time to get a move on.

Chapter 8.

The Chase.

Alex immediately grabbed Tom and Mia by the arms, "here a minute you two" pulling them away from the gathering, "look over there" Alex pointed to the two Chinese men dressed in black running up the hill. We have to get grandad back down the hill ASAP" said Alex. "My god" said Mia and immediately pulled from her handbag three of the small walkie talkie's grandad had put her in charge of. "Take these and head back to the pits, I'll handle things from here" said Mia with authority. She pressed the button on her walkie talkie and spoke. "Grandad, grandad do you read me over." "Loud and clear, over" came the tinny reply. "Two bogeys heading in your direction, Dolphis to stealth mode, head back to pits ASAP, over." "Message understood, over and out." Grandad replied.

Alex and Tom ran back to the pits where Uncle Lee was chatting with a motorcyclist friend. Alex sort of butted in and said "sorry Uncle Lee but can I talk to you for a minute?" "Sure Alex, excuse me for a moment Pete, now what's the trouble little man"

Alex thinking very quickly went on to say "Well grandads in a spot of bother, he err err yes that's right he got cut up the other day when he was out testing Spitty, "yes said Tom, and he was rather rude to them in his anger" "Was he now, rude to who?" said Lee wondering what was coming next. "Yes these two men just happened to be standing next to us as grandad went by up the hill and we overheard them say they where going to put grandads lights out" said Alex looking at Tom sideways. "Yea is there any thing you can do Uncle Lee" said Tom. "Ok" Lee said very slowly looking thoughtful with his hand on his chin. "You sure about this?" "Scout's honour" they both said with there fingers crossed behind their backs, looking very convincing. "Right-- so what do these chaps look like then? We don't want the old boy in any trouble do we?" "Oh thanks Uncle Lee," said Alex, they are two Chinese men dressed in black" and "they drive a black dodge van" added Tom. "How do you know all this then?" Said Lee concerned. "Grandad told us about it on the way here" said Alex as Tom nodded in agreement.

Lee looked at Pete and although looking a bit like hells angel dressed in his leathers was in fact a traffic cop. Pete removed his helmet and said "funnily enough we had a report only this morning, near where you boys live I think, a couple of Chinese guys acting suspiciously. I have a colleague working this beat in fact he's here today on duty, I'll go and see if I can find him." "Thanks Pete, by the way do you think I could use your Buell I want to nip up the back way to the top of the hill and check if grandads OK" said Lee. "No problem" said Pete and added "did any of you boys get the registration number of this van?"

"Yes its DHC 101X" said Tom reading from a piece of paper he pulled from his pocket.

"Right now you leave it to us" said Lee as Pete walked off to find his colleague.

Now here comes your Mum dad, wait here for grandad he will be with you safe and sound soon I promise." Tom and Alex went and stood over by old number 8 as Lee pulled on his helmet and started up Pete's Buell Firebolt motorcycle, he shouted to the boys over the engine noise "I'll talk to your Mum and dad when I get back" and within seconds he thundered off and was on his way up the hill to grandad.

Alex and Tom looked at each other rather sheepishly, "I do hope grandad and Dolphis are all right" said Alex gloomily. "Yea don't worry Alex, Mia's up there by now, and I bet she could beat those Chinese guys to death with her handbag, it weighs a ton you know."

They both laughed nervously as Mum and dad arrived. "Every thing all right you two, where's Mia?" "Oh she's gone for a walk to the top of the hill Mum" said Alex. "Oh! Ok I guess you three are as hungry as always then?" They all smiled as Mum opened a picnic basket in the back of the MG and pulled out four sandwich bags each with a name on and a large bottle of orange squash. Dad had a passion for egg sandwiches so his was double wrapped to keep in the pong. They all sat down on the grass behind the cars and made themselves comfortable, except dad who was jokingly told by Mum to move at least 10 feet away until he had finished the egg sandwiches. Alex felt the empty matchbox in his pocket with his left hand as he tucked into his cheese and tomato sandwich. I hope Dolphis and grandad are all right, he thought to himself. Both Tom and Alex nervously glanced up the hill several times as Mum handed out cups of orange squash, both unaware of the drama unfolding at the top of the hill.

Mia had stopped to catch her breath within several hundred yards of grandad, it was a hard climb up that hill and she was resting against a tree. She could see Lee had arrived and was circling grandad on the motorcycle keeping an eye open for trouble. Mia pulled out the walkie talkie and spoke into it, "grandad do you read"----- but that was all she had time to say, suddenly she was grabbed from behind and a hand was placed over her mouth, she struggled bravely but before she knew it the two Chinamen had bundled her into the back of the black van they had hidden in the trees, her hands were tied and a piece of tape placed over her mouth. "We swap you for Dragon ha ha ha" said Mr. Chang and laughed evilly." Mia kicked out as the two brothers exited the back doors and caught the younger one of them right up the bottom; he fell flat on his face into a thorn bush behind the van and squealed like a stuck pig.

Clambering to his feet he snarled back at Mia, "you pay for that young rady," Mia slunk back down her eyes wide open transfixed by his evil toothy grin, his gold teeth dispersed in his mouth like the black notes on a piano keyboard. Suddenly the older brother grabbed his raised arm and said "no time idiot brother" and slammed the back doors shut. He dragged his brother to the front of the van and opened the passenger door "You try anyring like rat again, I kick you in brackside too" he then slapped him round the head like a naughty boy and bundled him into the passenger seat.

Mr. Chang had picked up Mias handbag and the walkie talky dropped in the long grass, stuffing the handbag into the glove box he then ran round the front of the van jumped in his seat and started up the engine.

Alarmed grandad was standing up on his seat in the Bentley, his hand over the top of his eyes to shield them from the sun, trying to see what had happened down the hill. Dolphis was on grandads shoulder clinging onto his old leather jacket. Grandad beckoned to Lee and pointed down the track.

All three of them at the same time spotted the black van emerging from the trees heading strait for the old track that led back down to the pits. The van bounced out onto the rough road like a ping pong ball, constantly blowing its horn like a New York taxi driver and bits of grass and dust were billowing behind it as people and vehicles scrambled desperately to get out of the way.

"Mia's in there" shouted grandad, "Oh we have to help her" Dolphis lamented, "It's all my fault."

"Lee" shouted grandad, "do you think you could try and follow them down the track?" "Sure thing, I won't be able to get up much speed, but I'll do my best" said Lee.

"And see if you can get hold of your policeman friend, I think we are going to need him," grandad pointed to the finish line, "I'll go down the hill they will be opening it up any time now, my old bus wouldn't like that track to much" shouted grandad, "Oh and I'll radio the boys to meet me at the gate." "Right O, see you later" shouted Lee, as he roared off on the bike as fast as he dared. Grandad got strait on the walkie talky, "Tom, Alex are you reading me, over." Alex came back almost immediately, "what's up grandad? Over," "emergency test session—can you bring some fuel and meet me at the exit gate ASAP, over." "Will go, over and out" the reply was short and sweet.

Grandad knew the last qualifier had come up the hill so he started up Spitty to be first in line to go back down the hill. The dam red light was still on as the marshal on the finishing line waved his hand for them to slow down and stop. Come on- come on- come on, said grandad under his breath. But Dolphis had other ideas, suddenly the light turned to green, very much to the surprise of the marshal who had a very frightened look on his face as he jumped aside to avoid Spitty. Grandad floored the throttle and roared past the marshal in a cloud of acrid tyre and smelly exhaust smoke. Dolphis was still clinging on to grandad's jacket was nearly blown away as Spitty accelerated like a missile towards the first bend. Next the brakes were on as grandad pushed with all his might on the brake pedal sawing at the wheel and changing down a gear at the same time. While Spitty snaked into the corner like a rally car, Dolphis lost his grip and was thrown onto the dashboard and was sliding off to the left as they squealed round the right hand corner almost on two wheels. Dolphis held onto the dash with his claws and said a little prayer to the dragon gods. As grandad straitened up he could see the cloud of dust following the black van as it sped towards the pits, and it was only a few hundred yards from the exit gate. Spitty and grandad took the last left hander almost sideways and were now running parallel to the van.

Both drivers glanced over and looked at each other, both of them determined and bent over the steering wheels, but grandads luck was just about to run out.

Grandad looked up as they came blistering into the start line strait, two marshals in the distance where standing on the line waving danger flags frantically. Grandad sat up and stood on the brakes as hard as he could. Spitty's tyres squealed as he fought to control the skid, using all his skill he brought Spitty to a grinding halt several yards from the line.

The two marshals came running over as grandad watched the black van career out of the gate and escape into the countryside. "Dam and Blast it" grandad said banging his fist on the steering wheel and slumping back in his seat.

By now one of the marshals had run up to the side of Spitty and a little breathlessly exclaimed, "Woody old chap, (that was grandad's nickname to his racing friends) thank god you did not cross the line! There's oil all over the place down there. Some ones oil tank split, you would never had made the pit lane corner and crashed strait into the wall."

"Could you back up a little? We will take every one out of the emergency slip road gate till we get it cleared up."

Granddad composed himself and nodded; he carefully reversed Spitty back, and then drove forwards out through the emergency gate entrance.

As he chugged gently past the ambulance and fire truck crews attending to their respective vehicles, he could see Alex, Tom and Lee waiting for them on the grass by the side of the venue exit gate.

Grandad pulled over and they where joined by a police patrol car. Alex immediately leapt onto the side of Spitty. "Where's Dolphis grandad?"

"Oh dear in all that commotion I'd almost forgotten about him" grandad said as he started to look around the car. "I'm down here" said a tiny voice as Dolphis emerged from underneath the passenger's seat rubbing his head. "Are you Ok?" said Alex reaching down to pick him up. "Yes I'm fine," Dolphis said, "luckily I bounced on the seat before hitting the floor," still rubbing his head and obviously a bit shaken up, "that was a bit scary you know."

"I'm sorry about that old chap" grandad said seriously, trying not to laugh. Alex jumped into the front seat carefully placing Dolphis in his top pocket.

Everyone was arriving at the scene now and they had to think fast to try and explain what was going on. Tom was already strapping the spare cans of fuel onto Spitty as the two police officers got out of the patrol car. Grandad and Alex recognised them immediately as the two officers who had pulled them over, earlier that day.

Lee had got off the motorcycle and was now talking to grandad. "Look we have to tell Brian and Jenny," meaning the children's Mum and dad, "that Mia's been kidnapped."

The two officers now joined them and interrupted. "Now what's it all about eh Mr. Wood?" said the older policeman. "Thanks to Lee and my colleague Peter there's an all points bulletin out on this black van, Peter and the duty officer here at the track are in pursuit, but have not sighted it yet. Is there any more information you can give us sir?"

"Well err, it's err." Grandad's brain was going ten to the dozen.

"Yes it's because they think I'm an eccentric millionaire officer and err, they must be going to demand money or something in exchange for Mia."

"Right Sir kidnapping, this is very serious I am going to have to call in for some more back up."

Tom climbed into Spitty as the officer walked back to the patrol car and got strait on the radio. Grandad leant over the door towards Lee,

"Lee tell Brian and Jenny not to worry these men are not dangerous just stupid, me Alex and Tom are going to go after them."

"Is that wise? The police are not going to like it" said Lee.

"Don't worry about that, take this walkie talky and give it to your dad and Brian, tell them I am heading south west towards the old abandoned mines in the hills, and come yourself if you can borrow that bike, go on off you go and be quick about it."

"I hope you know what you are doing old man," Lee said as he turned and rushed over to the bike.

Grandad turned the ignition on "Ok boys stand by for take off, contact," and he pressed the starter. Spitty roared into life and within seconds they where thundering out of the gate towards the hills. The police and now attending onlookers watched in amazement as the old Bentley and crew disappeared in a cloud of dust and away into the distance.

Chapter 9

The Dragons tears.

The old Bentley almost flew along the winding narrow roads as the miles shot by. Grandad shouted out his instructions to Tom in the back. "Tom those roll maps in front of you, find the Devils Peak and tell me how many roads to it there are?" "Give me a few seconds grandad" said Tom. "Alex can you hold Dolphis in your lap but safe and secure mind, we are going to flush those kidnappers out and somehow set a trap for them." Grandad looked down at the instruments and tapped the fuel gauge. "Blast we need to top up on fuel; we'll pull in as soon as we can."

After a few more miles grandad slewed Spitty to a halt on a grassy edge which was surrounded by huge boulders that overlooked the valley below them. The other edge of the road dropped away down the steep hillside towards a river that was glinting in the sunshine as it snaked its way towards the sea. Grandad and Tom unlashed the cans of fuel and started to empty them into Spittys cavernous fuel tank. Alex in the meantime standing on his seat, kept a look out just in case. In no time Tom had resumed his map reading while grandad emptied the last can of fuel. "Corr that stuff stinks grandad" said Alex. "Sorry about that boys, but it did come from Uncle Ross's fish and chip shop before I added my special hydro carbon molecule fusion formula" he said proudly.

"Yea whatever grandad" said the boys raising their eyebrows and sniggering. "I wouldn't mind a drop of that" piped up Dolphis.

"This will! Blow your head off young Dragon so don't even think about it" said grandad with more than an air of caution in his words.

Dolphis slunk back down into Alex's hands looking quite sad.

"I'm really worried about Mia, sniffle, sniffle, it is all my fault" he said.

His head dropped and two little beads of golden tears formed in the corners of his eyes and dropped into Alex's hand.

Alex sniffled a little too, when suddenly the dragon detector machine in front of him started to go wild, hands spinning and trapdoors opening and closing like mad. "Grandad Grandad" Alex shouted. "I think something very strange is happening here, come and look." They all watched in amazement as the machine whirred and clanked like a crazy clock. "What the devils going on" said grandad.

"It's Dolphis's tears here look." Alex held out his hand to show them."

"Quick put them in the faraday cage." said grandad. Alex handed them to Tom and he quickly put them in the cage. The instrument stopped racing almost immediately, and with a clank and a click shut down closing the trap doors and going back to a random setting.

Grandad thought for several minutes pacing up and down beside the car. Then he stopped, "of course, of course! Dolphis, boys there's good news and bad news here. If you notice the machine's not registering Dolphis any more, so all of his electromagnetic energy must have been some how concentrated into those tears. The bad news is Dolphis I think you will have lost all your powers."

Both boys looked at Dolphis as grandads words hit home. "Oh my god Dolphis are you Ok?" Said Alex

"How do you feel?" Said Tom.

"I'm all right I think" and he scrunched his little eyes up concentrated hard, then coughed a few times, "your right I cant disappear and there's no sign of any smoke, but I feel fine" he said, trotting round in a circle in Alex's hands.

"I think" said grandad, pausing for a moment, "that Dolphis will only be able to recharge himself if he fly's through a thunder storm. And I recon we'll just have to leave that up to his Mum and dad, but all is not lost these tears have given me an idea. Don't worry little dragon we will get you home, I promise."

Grandad climbed back into his seat, clapped his hands and rubbed them together.

"Come on chaps we are going to lay a trap, let's get on with the battle plan. Tom what's the road situation?" Tom and Alex looked at each other and rolled their eyes, and without hesitation carried on with their tasks.

"Well it looks like there are two forks, the one we passed a mile or so back heading to—I think that farm down there and then on to the old mining town of Breswick. And the next fork right heading to, it says here abandoned mine works with the left fork carrying on through the hills to the coast and the town of Gwengoghley.

"Hmm I think this is going to be as good a spot as any. We have to contact Nigel Lee and your dad boys, and I'm a bit worried we haven't come across that police car yet, very strange, very strange indeed. Oh and Dolphis you'll be pleased to know, according to my calculations you home is round here on these very hills some where."

"I know I can feel it even though I've lost my powers." Said Dolphis, cheering up a little.

Grandad pulled out his little walkie talky twiddled with the knobs and started to speak.

"Come in Brian-Nigel-Lee--- are you receiving me? over."

The radio crackled. "Brian here, we are all assembled at the main crossroads that heads up into the hills, what's your situation? over."

"We are all OK here, and are going to leave what we think the kidnappers are after on a rocky outcrop about 3miles west of your position on the old Gwengoghly high rd.-over." "Understood, we have Pete and the police patrol here, they took the north road and found a broken down truck blocking the road, so the enemy must be up there with you somewhere" over. Granddad then said anxiously. "There are a lot of places to hide up here, so all we can do is to cut off their escape routes. But more importantly find Mia safe and sound, over."

"That's affirmative, we have alerted Gwengoghly police to lookout for the Dodge van, but we are all on our own up here for the moment, over."

"Ok Brian we are going to head up to the old abandoned mines, the kidnappers haven't contacted us yet but you can bet your bottom dollar they know we are right behind them, over."

Pete the police officer came on the radio. "Sir you be careful up there, don't take any unnecessary risks with those boys in tow, we are going to disperse and try and cover any escape routes. And keep in regular contact, is that clear? over."

"Loud and clear my friends lets radio in every 20mins, and good luck, over and out." Grandad eased himself back into his seat and put the radio back in his pocket.

"Well boys lets get on with it" he sighed. "Those Chinese guys are going to need a tank to get past us. Tom can you gather up Dolphis's tears and put them on those rocks over there? With a bit of luck they will think the tears are Dolphis and draw them out of hiding. I'll start up the car and we will then head up towards the old mines, everyone keep their eyes peeled ok." They all nodded silently and Dolphis took up his position behind the middle of the windscreen.

Tom leapt out and placed the tears of gold on the rocks and in a flash was back in his seat. Grandad pressed the starter and Spitty roared into life. Slipping Spitty into gear he let out the clutch and Spitty slithered back onto the narrow road with a squeal of tyres and the exhaust growling like a huge carnivores Dinosaur chasing its prey.

Spitty was now carrying the intrepid quartet towards perhaps danger, but most certainly to adventure.

Grandad worked hard at the controls of Spitty, slicing along the narrow winding roads heading towards the abandoned mines.

"Granddad look at this, your detector is starting to register." said Tom.

"Well we know it's not Dolphis we must be getting closer to your home young dragon." said grandad, as he expertly slid Spitty round another bend.

So while Alex and Dolphis peered through the windscreen looking for any signs of the kidnappers. Tom shouted instructions to grandad like a rally co driver. "Look out after the next bend, fork right and over the bridge."

Eventually a rickety old bridge came into view, and Spitty rumbled across the planking the whole structure creaking and groaning under the weight of Spitty and the crew. On reaching the other side they all breathed a huge sigh of relief but the road was getting rougher now and as they rounded the next bend it seemed to peter out towards what looked like an old quarry.

As they got closer several abandoned buildings came into view. "Look!" shouted Alex as Grandad heaved the brakes on. There it was, the black van, front doors open almost hidden between two buildings.

Cautiously grandad chugged towards the van as all pairs of eyes scoured the scene for any signs of life. They stopped, grandad turned the engine off, and the clatter of the handbrake ratchet sounded like a football rattle as grandad heaved it on. The silence was deafening as they all waited for something to happen.

"MIA" shouted grandad, but the only reply was an eerie echo, Mia---Mia----Mia.

A feeling of menace crept over the brave crew as the sun went in behind the black clouds that had started to form above them. The gathering storm had arrived completely unnoticed during the excitement of the chase and had now cast an eerie shadow over the whole scene.

Craw, craw, craw! The loud squawk of a crow echoed over the scene and made them all jump, adding to the ghostly silence and feelings of desolation and menace.

Suddenly the crackle of grandad's radio broke the silence. "Woody come in, Woody are you receiving me? over."

Grandad grasped his radio and spoke. "Receiving you loud and clear, over."

"What's your situation Woody? We are all in position here, over."

Grandad spoke cautiously. "All ok, continuing search will advise A.S.A.P. over."

Grandad put his radio back in his pocket and thought for a moment. "OK every body lets pull ourselves together. We'll have a thorough search of the area and keep as close together as we can, and be careful OK." They all nodded in agreement as Alex, Tom and Dolphis leapt out of Spitty with renewed enthusiasm.

The first target was the black van. Alex ran over and flung the rear doors open hoping against hope to find Mia, but of course it was empty. Alex turned round and sat between the open back doors of the van with Dolphis in his pocket.

Glumly he put his head in his hands. "What are we going to do?" he said. Tom sat down beside him and put his arm around him. "Don't worry little wiz we'll find her."

"If only I had some of my powers, I might just be able to detect her." Said Dolphis a little dejected.

The trio had reached a bit of low ebb while Grandad was busily checking the front of the van and the surrounding area. Suddenly he shouted excitedly. "Look there's another set of tyre tracks here, a big and heavy vehicle too, they are heading right down that rough track over there. So our Chinese friends have an accomplice eh."

Unexpectedly grandad's radio crackled again and he pulled it out of his pocket. This time it was the unmistakable voice of Mr. Chang.

"You think we stupid old man, ha ha ha."

Grandad snapped back, "If you have harmed that girl you will live to regret it Chang, OVER!"

"We hide girl in plenty good spot she fine, we detect your golden friend, we have him soon." The tone of Mr. Changs voice changed. "Just in case you try to stop us, we have remote gas bomb, make her very ill, ha ha ha. When we away flee and clear we tell, so no funny business o ke do ke."

Grandad was turning red with rage. "You! You! Ahhh." Grandad turned the radio off and flung it on the seat. He turned away from the boys his fists clenched muttering "give me strength" The boys had not seen grandad like this before and sat silently as his rage subsided.

Composing himself grandad picked the radio back up. Fiddling with the knobs he changed the channel. And without further hesitation he spoke. "All points come in. All points come in, over."

Pete answered. "Receiving you loud and clear, over."

"Pete did you pick up that last transmission, over?"

"Yes Mr. Woods and in respect of that last transmission from Mr. Chang, we will only shadow any suspect vehicle. We also have a search and rescue helicopter coming in from the west, but there's a big storm coming our way. Be careful, over."

Grandad replied with a more confident tone in his voice. "The enemy obviously can listen in to our transmissions, and with a bit of luck has not tuned in to this one yet. Contact Nigel and use Lee as a motor cycle courier to do this. Tell Nige I will be using our old code 9 for future transmissions. Nigel will brief you all on this, over and out."

Now code 9 was Grandad's and Nigel's reversal of information code with a bit of gobbledygook thrown in, simple but effective, in the short term.

And as always, the two old boys somehow instinctively knew what the other was saying. After all they had known each other for more than half a century.

Grandad gathered the boys around him. "Right boys and Dragon we have to act fast, I don't think the enemy knows we have found this spot. Dolphis your tears are taking them to where they think we are. We have to search this area thoroughly, before they get back O.K."

The team immediately leaped out of Spitty and started to work their way through the buildings, searching them one by one calling "Mia" as they went.

Eventually they came across a small building set apart from the rest and built into the Quarry face. The door on it had a huge padlock on it and was emblazoned with the words, DANGER EXPLOSIVES.

"This must be it" said Tom excitedly to Alex. Grandad shouted, "Mia are you in there?" but there was no reply. Pulling something from his pocket grandad started to fiddle with the padlock. Click, it flicked open. "Now stand back boys" he said as he unlatched the hasp and slowly opened the door. Tom and Alex stood behind grandad peering round him into the darkness as Dolphis climbed out of Alex's pocket and up onto grandad's shoulder. The tension was electric as grandad fumbled for the torch in his pocket. The beam penetrated the darkness but alas there was no Mia. Alex went inside and knelt on the floor. "Look what's this?" He picked up a rope and a piece of tape.

Tom shouted, "And here look."

"Don't touch it Tom" grandad retorted instantly. "It's the gas bomb." Tom stepped back and nearly trod on Dolphis who was quite at home in the dark. He was sniffing everywhere like a bloodhound. "OK everyone out" said grandad. "Let's regroup by Spitty as fast as we can." Alex picked up Dolphis and raced with Tom back to Spitty, grandad following up the rear as fast as his old legs could carry him.

They all gathered around Spitty a little out of breath but safe. "What now grandad?" said Alex. "Yes" said Tom.

Dolphis had now climbed right on top of Alex's head and was looking up at the black clouds swirling above them. "If only I had my powers?" he said sadly.

Grandad spoke up scratching his head "Well boys I think Mia was there, but she must have escaped or been taken some where else, it's a mystery we have to solve chaps."

"But the door was locked grandad, how could she have got out?" Alex said mystified.

"Mmmm." Grandad ran his hand through his white beard that had gathered quite a few dead flies on the journey. "While we think boys, let's refuel with a drop of ginger beer and some biscuits."

Grandad reached into the rear of Spitty and pulled out a flask of ginger beer and a packet of cream centred hobnobs. All of them still deep in thought took turns to swig from the flask and munch on the delicious biscuits.

Dolphis suddenly piped up. "Did you see that?" looking up and pointing with his claw at the clouds. "It was a flash of lightning, and I think I have an idea."

"Yes but you can't fly at the moment Dolphis" said Tom.

Dolphis ignored the remark. "Grandad I'm going to need some of your ginger beer please." "And Tom that small pipe over there, can you tap it into the ground as secure and upright as possible, right over there in that clear patch of ground? "Of course Dolphis but I don't understand" said Tom wiping the biscuit crumbs from his lips.

"You will" said Dolphis.

As Tom sprang into action Alex and grandad looked at each other realising what Dolphis's plan was.

"Alex" Dolphis continued, "I need a thin stick as straight as you can find about 2ft or 60cm long." "Right away" said Alex and immediately scampered off.

"Granddad." said Dolphis, "I hope you don't mind me calling you that?"

Grandad smiled. "I am honoured my little chap, now what can I do for you?"

"I have a problem I need a source of ignition, normally I click my gold teeth together and create a spark, but all my power has gone."

"That's easy." said grandad, and he bent down and opened a box on the side of Spitty in which he kept spares and tools. Rummaging through the box he pulled out a circuit tester. "Ah ha this has just the battery we need." He said opening the case and pulling out the battery.

"Now my little friend you see these two little terminals at the top, bite gently on those with your little golden teeth and when you release your grip there should be a tiny little spark."

"I see." said Dolphis smiling.

Before long everything was ready, Dolphis had drunk as much ginger beer as he could possibly hold, and was clamping himself with his claws onto the top of the stick Alex had found and placed under Dolphis's instructions into the tube that Tom had dutifully banged into the ground.

Dolphis had turned himself into a rocket. With his head facing downwards Dolphis folded his wings very close to his body and pointed his tail as strait as an arrow towards the sky. Alex knelt down beside him and stroked the back of his neck with his finger. "This is dangerous my little friend, please take care of yourself."

"Oh don't you worry about me I'll be back with my powers before you can say my name." and he winked at Alex.

"O.K. now, everybody stand back." said Granddad, and waited for the boys to be well clear.

He had tied the PP9 battery to the end of a long stick and was offering it to Dolphis at arms length just like he was lighting a real rocket.

"The storms right over head now young Dragon, go for it."

"This is going to be fun." said Dolphis, his eyes bulging as the huge burp built up inside him.

"I hope so." said grandad with his fingers crossed.

Dolphis closed his eyes and bit on the terminals. He released and instantly a red and blue flame erupted from his mouth and with a powerful whooshing crackling sound, he shot up towards the clouds like a shooting star. A trail of blue smoke marked his pathway to the sky as Alex sort of half waved watching his treasured friend disappear into the black clouds.

The excitement over Tom put his arm round Alex as they walked back to Spitty.

"That Dolphis is amazing eh little wiz." Alex smiled meekly.

It was with a mixture of excitement and sadness that they all climbed back into Spitty where they silently continued eating their biscuits and sipping grandad's ginger beer. All of them now deep in thought and watching the occasional flash of lightning, felt the first drops of rain falling.

After what seemed an age, grandad was the first to break the silence. "Ok boys give me a hand to put Spittys roof up."

No one spoke as they put on their rain jackets and helped grandad put up Spittys canvas hood.

The last poppers where fastened and with them all back inside Spitty the rain fell even harder. It fell on the canvas roof sounding like a herd of stampeding horses just above their heads.

Trying to break the mood of gloom Grandad suddenly perked up and said, "Right my lads it's no good sitting here, we have to do something."

"Yes but what?" Tom said.

"I just wish I knew where Dolphis was, I do hope he's ok" said Alex sadly.

"Mmmm" said grandad, "I am with you there but I am thinking we should take another look at that old explosives store, there's some thing there that doesn't add up. But we have to get rid of that rotten bomb thing first."

At last the rain was easing up now and Tom said "What's the plan then grandad?"

"Well Tom we are going to need a length of string, which by chance I just happen to have." Grandad fumbled in his old leather jacket pocket and pulled out a handful of all sorts of bits and bobs, amongst which was a coiled up piece of string. "Da daa." he said with a big grin on his face.

"What are you going to do with that?" said Alex perking up. "Well my intrepid pair we are going to--" grandad was stopped in mid sentence by a loud, bonk! The sound of something landing on Spittys roof, which made them all jump.

"Dolphis!" Cried Alex excitedly, "Is that you?" and to every ones delight Dolphis's little head appeared upside down looking in at them from the edge of Spittys hood with a huge smile on his face. He was steaming like a hot dog as the rain drops dripped down his little body and fell of the end of his snout.

"Dolphis!" they all shouted gleefully, and immediately Alex held out his cupped hands for Dolphis to drop into. "I might be a bit warmer than usual Alex." Dolphis chuckled as he dropped into Alex's waiting hands. Alex juggled Dolphis like a hot potato. "Oh, ow, ow," and then placed him on the top of the dash in front of him. "Are we glad to see you my little friend," said Alex blowing on his hands.

"Like wise my human family." said Dolphis stretching his wings and grinning like a Cheshire cat.

"How was it up there my little astronaut? You look fine to me." said grandad with a relieved smile upon his face.

Dolphis stood up on his hind legs and saluted. "Grandad I'm all recharged and reporting ready for action sir." The boys laughed as Grandad returned the salute.

"Right then men, there's no time to lose, let's get on with finding Mia then shall we?"

With renewed enthusiasm the reunited crew all got out of Spitty and gathered themselves together. Dolphis had cooled down a bit by now and was back in Alex's top pocket in the open matchbox looking out.

They all headed towards the old dynamite store while grandad explained his plan to remove the bomb.

"Dolphis Old chap now you are back with us; I am going to ask you to go into the Dynamite store and tie the end of this piece of string to the bomb, very carefully of course." "It's possible you could disable the bomb with your electrical powers but it could be booby trapped, so I don't think we should chance it, OK." "Once you are out of danger and free and clear I am going to pull the bomb clear and drag it out to that clearing in the trees over there." Grandad pointed to a spot several hundred meters away. "Are you ok with that Dolphis?"

"Yes Sir I understand," said Dolphis, climbing out of Alex's pocket into grandad's outstretched hand. "Boys, until I shout all clear, go and wait by Spitty, have you got that?" Alex and Tom nodded in agreement and ran off towards Spitty without hesitation.

Granddad put Dolphis on the ground and placed a loop of string in his mouth. Looking up grandad checked the boys where in position and well out of harms way.

"Ok Dolphis I'll give you plenty of slack and be careful I've no idea what's in that device?"

Dolphis disappeared into the darkness and grandad started to pay out string to give him as much distance as possible. Dolphis could see well in the darkness and a tiny red LED light blinking on and off on the bomb guided him like a beacon towards his task. Very carefully he tied the string around the shiny canister as secure as he could.

Satisfied his job was done he turned round and scampered out into the daylight. Granddad was waiting anxiously outside and had tied his old handkerchief over his nose and mouth. Dolphis instead of running off made several jumps and leaped towards grandad, gliding up and gripping onto his jacket. "I'm with you on this one alright" said Dolphis. "Glad to have you aboard, let's do it my friend."

Granddad took up the slack on the string and felt it go tight; gently he tugged on the line and could feel the weight of the dastardly device. "Let's hope we don't get snagged on anything, eh Dolphis." Moving slowly backwards grandad could feel the bomb being dragged by the string. Very carefully they continued and the bomb was soon out through the door. "So far so good." Said grandad wiping the beads of sweat from his forehead with his hand. He paid out the last length of string and checked the wind was blowing away from all of them, just in case it went off.

"Right, it's now or never." said grandad and he started walking backwards at a steady pace dragging the bomb towards the clearing.

After several minutes grandad and Dolphis where backing their way into the undergrowth. At last they felt it was far away enough to pose little threat to their exploration of the dynamite shack and surrounding area.

Giving the bomb a wide birth grandad and Dolphis made their way back and waved at the boys still patiently waiting by Spitty. "All clear!" grandad shouted, and the boys eagerly ran to greet them at the empty explosives building.

At least the storm had past over and the sun was making a welcome appearance again as the team gathered together by the door. Although called a shack the explosive store was in fact very strongly built on solid rock.

Grandad pulled out his radio. "I'm going to check in with Nigel but don't take any notice of what I say, OK crew." They all nodded and started to explore the area.

Dolphis had climbed down from grandad and was already investigating the inside of the building. "Can we borrow your torch grandad?" said Alex, as they peered into the darkness.

"Yes but be careful though you two." Granddad handed them the torch and they disappeared through the door. He fiddled with the radio and spoke, "Nige, come in Nige, over."

A few seconds past and Nigel's voice replied. "Reading you loud and clear, over."

Grandad spoke carefully and clearly. "Calling off search—all is lost---Queen in no danger--- do not entertain mad hatter, over" .Nigel replied, "X marks the spot--- black rhino spotted, over." "Understood over and out"

What grandad had actually said to Nigel was. "Continuing search, all ok but Mia could still be with the kidnappers. In reply, Nigel told grandad, a large black 4X4 was spotted where they had left Dolphis's tears. Grandad popped the radio back in his pocket and was deep in thought when suddenly an excited cry came from Alex inside the building.

"Grandad come and look at this!" He rushed in to find Alex and Tom crouching round a large stone slab in the floor, Dolphis was jumping up and down excitedly in the middle of it, his little tail wiggling and flapping his wings. "I can smell dragons, I can smell dragons" he chanted, leaping higher and higher almost beside himself with excitement.

Grandad picked up a stone and tapped the stone slab. "Well it certainly sounds hollow to me." Before he could utter another word and as if by magic the huge stone started to move. "Stand back every body." grandad shouted calmly, and he pulled Tom and Alex away from the slab. First it dropped down gently recessing itself into the floor rumbling and crunching as it went, the little dragon was still jumping and running round in circles on the slab, this time exclaiming even more excitedly, "There here! There here! There here! "Dolphis be careful" shouted Alex, but grandad held Alex back as he tried to reach down and rescue Dolphis. "He'll be ok don't worry." said grandad. The stone stopped with a thud, and then grating and grinding like an old millstone it started to slide sideways underneath the floor. Grandad shone the torch into the dark hole that was being revealed, and they could just make out a series of small steps leading down into the darkness. Dolphis immediately jumped onto the first step. "Come on you lot! Mia must be down here some where, it's got to be a secret way into my lair, I mean home." he said with a huge grin on his face.

"That would explain a lot" said grandad. "But if we follow you young dragon we are going to be at a bit of a disadvantage, our radio will not work down there."

"Trust me I have a good feeling about this and there's no time to lose my friends" said Dolphis still jumping up and down. Tom and Alex were now getting quite excited.

"Yes come on grandad."

Grandad nodded in agreement, "Ok you guys but I will radio in first and we are going to need some light, this little torch won't last long down there and we can't see as well as you in the dark, young dragon."

"Ok, ok, ok, I'm sorry it's just that I am so excited I can't wait to find Mia and see my Mum and dad again." said Dolphis.

"I can't wait to see your Mum and dad either." said Tom raising his eyebrows and grinning at Alex. The tension was broken and they all laughed as they forgot for a moment the ensuing danger of the dragon hunters who weren't going to give up the prize of a golden dragon easily.

Chapter 10.

Breaking the Rules.

Grandad pulled out his radio and told Nigel in his usual back to front gobbledegook their plan. And that if they had not heard from him in 60 minutes, the team should converge at the dynamite shack, making sure the police had blocked all exit routes.

Nigel tried to talk grandad out of going underground, not knowing of course that grandad and the boys had Dolphis as a guide and although secondary to finding Mia, Getting Dolphis back to his parents was part of the plan. Grandad signed out with "don't worry we'll be fine." and ushered the boys and Dolphis back over to Spitty.

Grandad started removing one of the rear lights from Spitty and asked Tom to fetch some spare batteries he had stowed for the communication radios. Within minutes and with the help of some bits of string wire and tape, grandad was fixing the lamp and bulb to his old flying helmet. He taped the batteries to his belt where the wires dangling from the helmet were held in contact by a couple of elastic bands.

Jokingly he modelled his newly fashioned head ware like a catwalk queen. "There, what do you think of that boys? Not perfect but it will do."

"That's fantastic grandad, but why don't we just light some sticks or something?" said Alex, quizingly.

"Well my boy, it is possible that in some of these old mines pockets of gas can build up with explosive results if we walk into them with a naked flame. In the old days miners had a thing called a Davis lamp, a bit like Dolphis's Faraday cage here, but instead of a dragon you had a flame in it. Alex was listening intently and made a mental note to ask grandad about Faraday cages and things when they weren't quite so busy.

Grandad continued, "But that's not all, in the old days the miners used to take Canary's in cages down the mines with them too." "Canary's!" said Tom, "whatever for?"

"Canary's are particularly sensitive little birds to a change in air quality and they would stop singing, feint and fall off their perch, alerting the miners that there was danger."

"Did they die?" said Alex sadly. "Yes I rather think some of them did, but they did save the lives of many men. I am afraid they didn't have the sophisticated electronics we have today boys. And unfortunately we haven't either, but we do have young Dolphis here." said grandad, leaning forward and smiling at Dolphis as he peered out of Alex's top pocket. "You will let us know if you detect a change of air or anything young Dragon won't you" said grandad.

"Of course my friends, I'll sing like a Canary" said Dolphis chuckling.

"Uhhhhh" the boys retorted. "But I thought that was really funny" said Dolphis looking bewildered and slightly hurt.

Instantly they all burst into laughter pointing at Dolphis and for a few moments they couldn't even speak, they all just laughed. In the end Dolphis realised they were just having fun with him and joined in the laughter puffing little smoke rings from his nostrils uncontrollably, which just made the whole crew laugh even more.

"O dearie, dearie me" said grandad as the laughter died down, "I'm all out of breath now, Right you bunch of comedians." he said pulling himself up to attention ,"we have a job to do here, lets get on with it."

The seriousness' of the task now covered them all as they marched back to the dynamite shack, grandad talking as they walked.

"Dolphis and Alex you two take pole position. Dolphis I guess you can bound ahead in front of us and warn us of any danger. Tom you next and I'll follow up the rear."

The explorer's entered the darkness of the dynamite shack and proceeded to enter the hole in the ground carefully climbing down the steep steps. Dolphis first then Alex, Tom followed while grandad shone his light so they could all see. Carefully they edged downwards and just before he disappeared, Grandad wedged an old piece of wood across the opening keeping the exit open, just in case.

At the bottom of the steps the ground sloped slightly downwards into a tunnel and although grandad had to stoop a little it was quite passable.

The tunnel had been cut from solid rock and the damp rough edges glistened in the light of grandad's torch as they weaved their way silently into the labyrinth.

While every one else's eyes were slowly getting used the darkness. Dolphis was bounding backwards and forwards like a miniature otter in his excitement. The tunnel was opening up a bit now and slowly they made there way through occasionally having to dodge groups of white stalagmites hanging from the ceiling. Touching their hands on the sides as they past through, the tunnel twisted and turned but always they were slowly heading downwards.

Although the floor was wet and had the occasional puddle under the stalagmites, the gravel surface was not too slippery and it was surprisingly warm, and getting warmer as they continued on.

Since they had entered the tunnels only the sound of the odd drip of water, and the sound of their footsteps crunching and splashing through the tunnel had broken the eerie echo like silence.

Suddenly the tunnel split in front of them and they halted, Dolphis bounded up and sniffed around the two entrances. Alex spoke up, "Which way Dolphis?" Alex's words echoed eerily around them. "WHICH WAY DOLPHIS, WHICH WAY Dolphis, WHICH way Dolphis, Dolphis, Dolphis." A little shiver went down Alex's spine and he turned and gripped Tom's hand. "Whoa that was a bit spooky Tom."

"Don't worry little wiz I'm right here." Alex gave Tom a nervous smile and both brothers new instinctively that this knew bond that had formed between them would always be there. "I guess we both will, that is, be here for each other I mean, thanks to Dolphis." Alex whispered.

Grandad spoke up softly, "OK guys I'm going change batteries, Tom can you get out the little torch?"

"Yes" said Tom. Immediately Dolphis bounded up to grandads feet "I'll give you some light, there's no gas down here."

"Right you are, my little friend," said grandad "go for it."

Dolphis sat up and blew gently through his nostrils and two white flames appeared. "That's so cool Dolphis." said Alex. Dolphis looked up at him and winked as the flickering flames lit up the tunnel. Grandad changed the wires over on the batteries while Tom and Alex looked around; Alex's sharp eyes had seen something on the wall.

"Hey what's this?" he exclaimed moving closer and rubbing his hands on the wall. They all moved in to get a closer look as grandads light came on again. "It looks like some sort of hieroglyphics." said grandad, and he picked up Dolphis from the floor to give him a better look at the strange looking letters.

"Oh my! I'm excited now, that's dragon speak that is, I must be close to home." said Dolphis trying to contain himself. "Well what do's it say Dolphis?" said Tom excitedly.

"Oh let me see now, I m r o n t o w – imrontow, YES! It says way out, and its pointing the way we've just come! Yippee yaroo we can't be far now."

Dolphis excitedly did a little dance around grandad's hand and leaped down onto the floor of the tunnel.

"Which way now Dolphis? Lets get a move on." said Alex.

"Right, we go right, I can sense it we are near to Mia."

The brave crew moved on with a renewed sense of urgency and excitement as they headed off down the right hand side branch of the tunnel.

But what they didn't know was that back up on the surface a big black Hummer containing not just Mr. Chang and his brother, but the master mind of this whole grizzly kidnap affair. A heinous criminal by the name of Hiram Spode, nick named 'The Toad'. The kidnappers had driven up the side of the valley through the trees and undergrowth avoiding the roadblocks. And they where rumbling in this monster of a 4X4 towards the dynamite shack. Where it seems the Chang brothers had imprisoned Mia earlier, or at least thought they had.

Hiram was still fuming that they had been duped by grandads plan and the golden tears, as the big black hummer pulled up opposite the dynamite shack.

Now Hiram was a most disagreeable man and most aptly named on account of his huge size and fat face, always sweating, his pock marked features really did resemble an amphibious Toad. Hiram having spent most of his criminal life smuggling illicit Chinese goods, and despite his huge bulk was a most elusive and secretive man.

The authorities had tried many times to catch him but he had always managed some how to escape.

Seeing the door had been opened on Mia's prison he spat out at Mr. Chang. "You idiots!! they must have got the girl back, we have lost everything now. Imbeciles go and check the dynamite shack."

The Chang brothers leaped out of the hummer, nearly falling over each other in their haste to avoid more of the Toads venomous words.

Hiram edged his great bulk out of the hummer and slowly surveyed the scene as the clumsy pair of brothers ran to investigate the shack. Waddling ungainly towards the shack, he spotted Spitty. "Wait you fools! Perhaps all is not lost, they must still be here some where, but why have they not made their getaway and escaped?"

"Go and check that old car and every building, forget about the girl I want that Dragon. Come on hurry up fools." he shouted menacingly.

The two brothers stopped in their tracks turned round and bowed slightly. "Yes master." they said, and scuttled off towards Spitty.

Hiram by now was hatching an ambush plan in his head, and if they where to return to Spitty he wanted to be ready. He ambled back to the hummer and squeezed himself back into the drivers' seat. He started it up and proceeded to reverse it back into the trees. If the brothers where to flush them out, he would be ready, he thought.

Settling back in his seat he took a handkerchief from his pocket and mopped the beads of sweat running down his face. Slipping the handkerchief back in his pocket his fat fingers reached for a big cigar resting in the ashtray.

He lit it up and puffed several times, still keeping his big beady eyes watching out for any sign of his golden pay cheque. He now reached into his top pocket and pulled out the two golden tears left by grandad on the rocks below. Greedily he imagined the fortune that was almost in his grasp and a sly selfish grin spread slowly across his ugly fat face.

Meanwhile down below, grandad and the boys hadn't gone more than 50 paces into the right hand tunnel when a loud thud echoed round their ears stopping them in their tracks.

It was the stone door closing in the dynamite shack, grandad gathered the boys close to him as they stood in silence, waiting for something to happen.

Tom and Alex looked worried as grandad put his finger to his mouth, "shoosh" he said quietly, "listen." Dolphis came scuttling back and climbed up onto Alex's shoulder and whispered. "Don't worry if it's those kidnappers I'll give them a welcome they won't forget." Dolphis leapt down and stood upright in the tunnel guarding his friends like a soldier.

Something was coming towards them; they could hear the sound of several footsteps and the splash of water getting closer and closer. To cap it all grandad's headlight suddenly flickered out and plunged the crew into pitch darkness. Granddad fumbled to fix it cursing under his breath while Tom and Alex huddled closer and gripped him like a pair of limpets. The light flickered several times when suddenly Dolphis let out a piercing cry. They all jumped out of their skins as he shouted

"DAD!" Tom by now had clumsily got out his little torch, switching it on he shone it over Dolphis's head and there coming towards them was a big version of Dolphis.

"Please don't be alarmed my friends I am here to help you." said the dragon walking towards them. Dolphis by now was dancing like a puppy around his dad stopping to give him a big hug. "This is my dad, are we glad to see you."

"Like wise my son, so this must be the Woods boys then?" said the big dragon looking up at Grandad Tom and Alex.

They where still a little stunned at facing a very much bigger version of Dolphis.

"My name is Dolphim and you must be Alex, Tom and Mr. Woods senior.

They relaxed as at last grandad's headlight come on, showing Dolphim in all his splendour. "Mega cool." uttered Tom as grandad reached his hand down.

"Very pleased to meet you Sir." grandad said shaking Dolphim's clawed hand.

Without hesitation Dolphim spoke. "There is no time to waste my friends and we have a guest who can't wait to see you all, follow me if you will gentlemen." He squeezed past them all and headed off in the direction they had been going. "Oh and by the way thank you for bringing Dolphis back to us." He said looking back at them.

"What about the kidnapper's" said Alex, running to keep up with Dolphim, "won't they try and follow us?"

"Don't you worry about that young Sir we have everything under control." said Dolphim confidently as he led them onwards.

The mood among the whole family was now one of euphoria as the narrow tunnel opened up into a huge cavern lit by strange glowing rocks, and there just on the other side sitting between several Dragons was Mia.

Immediately she jumped up and they all ran towards each other.

Amidst tears and cries of joy and laughter a big group hug ensued. "I was a bit scared grandad but I new you would save me," sniffing back the tears and giggling nervously, "I love you guys."

"We are just happy to find you my dear." said grandad.

"Echo that" said Alex and Tom, Both of them beaming from ear to ear.

"Come and meet Dolphis's Mum" said Mia wiping the tears away with her hand.

Mia took Alex and Tom by their hand's and led them over to where she had been sitting.

Little Dolphis was already there snuggling up to his Mum and they both looked very happy indeed.

"This is Dolpher; she is the one that found me in that terrible shack the kidnappers put me in."

Mia smiling sat down beside Dolpher and put her arm around her. Dolphis bounded over to Mia and sat on her lap. Wiggling his tail and smiling up at Mia he said, "You are so brave Mia, I am so sorry you got into danger because of me." Mia blushed a little reached down and patted him on the head.

Dolpher beckoned to the boys, "Come and sit beside me boys," she said in a soft dragon voice, "Mia has told me so much about you."

The two boys sat in front of her still a little dazzled, she was indeed a beautiful dragon and spoke gently as she told them of how she had found Mia, by a pure accident.

"I was searching the tunnels just in case Dolphis had managed to find his way home. When I heard the sound of someone sobbing, of course I went into invisible mode and investigated. Some how I knew Mia and Dolphis where connected, call it a mothers instinct. When I revealed myself to Mia she knew who I was straight away.

And when Mia told me the story, well! At last, here we all are, safe and sound." Dolphis trotted over to his Mum and whispered something in her ear. She smiled and said, "Yes of course my dear."

Grandad in the meantime on the other side of the cavern was deep in conversation with Dolphim, no doubt hatching some sort of plan.

"Yes" said grandad, "in about 20 minutes those kidnappers will get a bit of a surprise, but I would like if I can, to get the surface and tell Nigel and the police that Mia is safe and sound."

"I think that can be arranged Mr. Woods, the children will be quite safe down here and perhaps," Dolphim said with a cheeky smile on his face, "We could warm things up a bit for Mia's assailants as well. Now about that ginger beer you where talking about, do you have some on you?"

"Never go any where without it." said grandad laughing and reaching into his knapsack.

Dolphim gestured to several of the dragons that had been shyly hiding amongst the rocks and a small group soon gathered around Dolphim and grandad.

Granddad reached into his knapsack to get out the flask of ginger beer and felt a large bar of chocolate he had put in there. "Mia" he shouted, "I'm sorry my dear I had forgotten in all this excitement you must be very hungry, grandad pulled it out and waved it in the air.

"I'll get it for you." said Alex, and he jumped up from her side and ran over to grandad. "Oh and there's another flask of ginger beer here for you as well." grandad handed them to Alex, who turned round and hopped skipped and jumped his way back to Mia casually dancing on the rocks on his way. Suddenly Dolpher shouted "STOP ALEX WAIT" but it was too late he just disappeared.

Tom and Mia let out a gasp, as grandad ran to the spot. Dolpher then shouted calmly. "Don't worry he's perfectly fine he's just found our forth dimension room. Dolphis and I where just about to take you children there anyway, come on let's go and join him."

Tom and Mia walked apprehensively with Dolpher over to the large smooth round pebble like stone where Alex had seemingly vanished. "All you have to do is jump on it with both feet, It's quite safe I promise you." said Dolpher.

"Dolphis you go first I'm sure Alex will be pleased to see you." Dolphis jumped on the stone and promptly disappeared. "Tom you next" said Dolpher. "I'm a bit worried about this" said Tom hesitating, "don't be silly" said Mia and gave him a shove.

Tom closed his eyes and just stepped onto the stone, but he didn't disappear. "You have to jump with both feet." said Mia, "oh all right." said Tom shakily and tried again.

This time he vanished and to his great surprise found himself in a cave standing on another smooth stone, but now he was surrounded by all manor of gold objects and amongst them, neat piles of golden gleaming dragon skins filled every nook and cranny. Tom stepped off the stone rubbing his eyes in disbelief. Alex still in a state of trance was sitting on a golden seat still holding the bar of chocolate and flask of ginger beer, with Dolphis sitting proudly on his lap. The boys both looked at each other. "Wow" said Alex; "Double wow." said Tom. "Look at those up there." said Alex, pointing to rows of neat rectangular holes cut in the rock. Each had a single perfect gold dragon skin placed inside them. A few seconds later Mia and then Dolpher appeared. Mia just stood there totally amazed as Dolpher casually strolled up to the boys and sat down in front of them.

"It's all quite beautiful isn't it." she said "It's a shame we have absolutely no real use for all this gold. Except that we like to amuse ourselves and some times make pretty things out of it. You see children; we shed our skins once every five years in order to grow."

"You mean like a snake?" said Tom.

"Yes that's exactly right" said Dolpher chuckling. Mia came over and sat beside the boys still speechless. Alex pointed up to the boxes high on the walls of the cave. "Why are those up there?" he said.

"Ah well" said Dolpher, "each one of those is the last skin we shed before we go on to the fifth dimension." She pointed up to a skin on the far side. "That's my great, great, great, great, great, great grandfather over there. He sailed with the Vikings you know. We love to come down here and tell stories about our ancestors." Dolpher said proudly.

The three children where transfixed and listened intently as Dolpher continued telling her story. "I'm afraid all this gold is really our curse and without it we would be just another animal. The great wizard gave it to us eons ago, as protection from the elements. So we could use our powers for good but when humans found out how rare and valuable it was, they almost wiped us out and so it is still the same today. You won't tell anybody about us, will you children."

Alex stood up followed by Tom and Mia, "I speak for all three of us." said Alex very seriously. "We promise on our lives and with our hearts that we shall never reveal any of the secret things you have told us and will always be ready to help our dragon family in any way we can, oh and that includes grandad as well."

All three of them placed their hands one on top of the other and leant down towards Dolpher who stood up on her hind legs and added her hands to the pledge.

Dolphis not to be left out, leapt onto the bunch of hands and wrapped himself around them. "Don't forget me" he cheerily butted in. "How could we." said Alex jokingly and they all laughed together.

"This breaks our dragon rules a little bit" said Dolpher "but I think at last it's time to forge a friendship with the human world again. "We won't let you down" said Tom. "I'll make sure of that" said Mia. "Friends!" Said Dophis gleefully, "I am so happy."

"I think it's time we returned to the others children, our council want to meet you and thank you for helping my precious Dolphis here." Dolpher smiled up at them all and gently ushered them all back over to the big smooth stone.

Tom turned round for a last look around, and was still a bit hesitant about using this new form of transport, thinking to himself, I must be dreaming.

Each one in turn they jumped on the stone and duly disappeared, finding them selves back in the main chamber where it seems the whole family of dragons had gathered to meet them.

They all walked slowly over to a gathering of dragons which had formed up close to a tunnel leading to a series of steps. Alex noticed a particularly large and imposing dragon beckoning them to come closer. Dolphis had taken up his usual position on Alex's shoulder and whispered in his ear, "That's Drockfost our leader."

"Oh right." said Alex quietly.

The children sort of nodded and said hello to each dragon as they past the line up, all the dragons smiled shyly back as they got closer to Drockfost. Suddenly a tiny little dragon bounded out in front of Mia. The precession stopped, Mia bent down and said gently "Hello little dragon." The little dragon spoke in a tiny little voice.

"You're a girl human aren't you, and can I feel your hair?"

"Of course" said Mia giggling, and offered her hand to the little dragon.

"Fismis!.... Oh dear I am so sorry." said the little dragons mother stepping forward. "She's always getting into trouble."

Mia replied "It's no trouble at all; she is such a beautiful little dragon." Mia picked up Fismis and gathered her long black hair from over her shoulder, and placed the strands in front of Fismis sitting on her hand. "There little Fismis help yourself."

The little dragon said "Thank you." and buried her head in Mia's hair disappearing for a moment and then popping her head up. "Oooh it's so soft and bendy just as I had imagined" and she disappeared again. A gentle laugh rippled round the cavern as all the dragons watched Fismis revel in this new experience.

Drockfos now spoke up and said in a deep and calming voice. "Children and dragons would you all please follow me up into our ceremonial chamber. When you are ready of course," bowing his head towards Mia.

Mia carefully handed back Fismis to her mother. "Goodbye Fismis, perhaps you and your Mum can come and visit me later?" Mia winked, kissed her finger and placed it on Fismis's head. "I have to go now she whispered."

The three children then moved forward and followed Drockfos through the tunnel entrance. As they steadily climbed the steps they could see the flickering light of a flame high above them which seemed to lead to a large bright chamber.

As they got closer to the top finally they could see a huge stone bowl supported on three tall pillars at the back of a golden chamber. The flames flickered gently in the bowl casting the light and reflecting in the rock walls a warm golden glow. The chamber was neatly surrounded by a row of sugarloaf shaped stone seats and several dragons where already in place as the entourage entered.

Drockfos beckoned the children to stand on a large flat flagstone decorated with inlayed golden designs and hieroglyphics.

Drockfos then climbed up and sat down on a larger stone seat in front of the big stone bowl. By now all the dragons that had followed them had found a seat around the chamber. With the children now standing in front of him gazing around, Drockfos spoke again.

"Friends, there are several persons not here whom we shall honour later, namely, Mr. Woods snr and Dolphim, who at this moment in time are engaged on other urgent business." A little ripple of laughter went round the congregation at this remark.

"Now to the reason we are here." "Tom Alex and Mia, our council has decided to present each of you with a special gift." "These will link you to us in more ways than you thought possible." All the dragons clapped in agreement. Drockfos held up his hand asking for silence. He then gestured to a dragon on his right who was holding a golden box to come forward. "Let me explain children."

Drockfos opened the box to reveal four slim beautifully made gold cases. "Mia come forward please." Mia stepped forward and Drockfos lifted out the first case opening the lid as she stood in front of him. Inside was an incredible solid gold miniature dragon, held between chains of wonderful complexity.

Mia's sharp intake of breath echoed round the silent chamber and for a few seconds Mia was unusually lost for words. "Oh it's so beautiful." she exclaimed.

"That's not all." he replied, and he pressed on a tiny tab hidden in the decoration on the side of the box. A secret lid sprang open in the corner and a gold ring with a black dragon emblem inscribed on it emerged. The ring shone like a twinkling star reflecting the flames burning in the great bowl behind him. Drockfos lifted it out and offered it to Mia.

"This my dear is the key, both these objects have been made from the tears of dragons collected over hundreds of years. Each pendant endows its wearer with one of our dragon powers, and yours my dear will give you the power to read minds. An excited hum went round the seated dragons and they all clapped in appreciation.

"Thank you Sir." said Mia humbly fighting back a little tear.

Tom and Alex looked at each other amazed as Drockfos gestured to Tom to come forward. Handing him the next open case, he said. "And yours Tom will give you the power to manipulate electrical things."

"Well cool!--- I mean thank you Sir." said Tom stepping back and bowing his head.

"And now Alex...please" Alex stepped forward still with Dolphis sitting proudly on his shoulder. "Alex, for such a young human you have shown great bravery and concern for us dragons particularly, and we are happy to give you the power of invisibility."

Alex beamed. "Thank you very much indeed sir." excitedly he turned and hugged his brother and sister thanking Drockfos and all the dragons once again.

He added, "You know we are going to have to tell our Mum and dad about this, could Dolphis come and stay with us for a little while? All the dragons laughed and Drockfos raised his hand again to bring order while trying not to laugh himself.

"We will see, but there is more you should know my honouree Dragon friends." "As you see, each golden dragon has a ring that goes with it, and the powers will only work if you are wearing both at the same time, all you have to do is touch them together and the power is activated. Touch them together again and you are back as you where, simple."

Drockfos put on a sterner face. "With these powers come great responsibility you know, but you can have some fun as well. But misuse them and you will get a visit from us, understand."

"Of course Sir, Yes." they all nodded and said in unison.

"Excuse me Sir, but could I ask what power you have given Granddad." Alex said quizingly.

Drockfos smiled. "Well-- we couldn't really decide and in view of his outstanding contribution to getting little Dolphis here home." And he blew a tiny smoke ring at Dolphis still sitting on Alex's shoulders. "We gave Granddad's talisman ALL of our powers."

"Whoa!" said Tom. Granddad is going be well pleased." All the Dragons clapped and cheered. The children danced on the spot as they clasped hands then slowly each in turn bowed and clapped back mouthing, "thank you, thank you."

As the excitement calmed down Drockfos raised his arms again and spoke out.

"Speaking of Mr. Wood's children I think its time you were on your way home. I sense Dolphim and your grandfather is bringing your adventure to a close on the surface."

The children thanked all the Dragons again as they gathered round to celebrate this new alliance forged in friendship and trust.

Eventually they all started to make their way back down the steps. Mia was surrounded by several dragons, chatting away ten to the dozen answering questions and showing everyone her ring and talisman. Tom was talking to Drockfos about his computer games and nearly fell over in amazement when Drockfos said he could remember watching the Great Wall of China being built.

Alex meanwhile was still standing by the big stone bowl as the chamber emptied.

He stood looking into the flames with Dolphis quietly sitting on his shoulder. There where no words to be said, they both knew they would have to be saying goodbye soon. Alex tried to cheer them both up.

"I am sure we'll be able to see each other again soon, grandads always nipping up to see uncle Nige."

"Yes." said Dolphis "we've had quite an adventure together haven't we." and nuzzled his warm little head against Alex's cheek.

"Come on you two we haven't got all day." Tom shouted back at them. Alex took a deep breath popped Dolphis back in his top pocket and ran to catch up with his brother. The departing crowd where now noisily entering the main chamber. Mia had linked up with little Fismis and her mum once more.

Chapter 11.

A Warm Welcome.

Meanwhile on the surface, grandad, Dolphim and several of his cousins had emerged from a hidden entrance near the abandoned mine buildings. They could hear the Chang brothers rummaging around and cursing as they searched in the semi darkness of an old kitchen building just a few meters away.

The younger brother was wide eyed and a bit scared as he searched though the debris and old pots and pans that littered the floor. Carelessly he flung an old saucepan to one side hitting his brother on the head as he bent down to look under an old plank of wood. Bong! "Ohhww you crumsey irriot bruvver, why you no watch out? He said rubbing his head and sucking air in through his teeth.

"Sorry, what you think I have eyes in back of head," he replied sarcastically.

Without even thinking about it, the older brother picked up the offending saucepan and swung it back at his brother catching him on the back of the head.

Bong! "Ahaa now you have bump on back of head instead of eyes, irriot."

It was certain now that the two brothers where just about to engage in a fist fight.

When, Granddad's silhouette appeared at the door holding what looked like a gun, but in truth was just a knarled old piece of stick. His words stopped them in their tracks.

"Good afternoon gentlemen, having a bit of a disagreement are we?"

The two brothers panicked and almost fell over each other while scrambling to get out of the other door. They almost jammed each other in the door frame as they fell out into the sunlight and broke into a run while attempting to escape.

This of course was perfect timing as Nigel Lee and the rest of the rescue squad headed by the police car had just crossed the old bridge and were heading in the direction of grandad, who had just previously radioed in his position. But there was just another little surprise waiting for them.

The two brothers spotting the convoy coming towards them cutting off their escape route skidded to a halt. Only to be treated to a quick blast of flame on their backsides coming from an invisible Dolphim and two other dragons that had followed behind them. The pair now ran even faster patting their backsides to try and quell the flames, crying "help us, help us," the comical pair headed strait into the waiting arms of the two policemen, who promptly rolled them on the ground to put out the smoke and flames.

As soon as they where able a pair of handcuffs where snapped on their wrist's behind their backs by the policemen. The two slightly singed brothers although relived started to whinge and wriggle on the ground. "It was him, he made us do it." They bleated and nodded their heads towards the Hummer hidden out of view. The policemen looked up but could see nothing.

He then waved his hand in front of his face "cor that pongs a bit." Pointing to the scorched trousers that where still smoking a little.

"Better get the fire extinguisher out son." he said to his very young colleague, and nodded towards the patrol car.

The two brothers where duly hosed down by the fire extinguishers adding further to their humiliation but still protesting their innocence. Eventually the policemen helped them up and the two brothers where looking very sorry for themselves as everyone gathered round. "OK let's get them in the car and read them their rights then." said the officer.

Brian Nigel and Lee butted in pointing at the two brothers. "Where are the children?" said Brian. "Yes and where's the old man? I can see Spitty over there." said Nigel.

The China men just shrugged their shoulders, hung their heads and said nothing as they where helped into the police car.

"HERE WE ARE" was the shout from behind the building, as the slight frame of grandad and a bunch of smiling children emerged.

Every one turned round to look amidst a cry of relief from Mum. "My babies." she cried with her arms wide open.

While all this had been going on grandad had gone back to the secret entrance and picked up Mia, Tom and Alex who had been brought to the surface by Drockfos.

"Go on kid's take this knapsack containing you know what, and run to your Mum and dad. Dolphim and I have just got one more thing to take care of."

Grandad winked at them all and strode off to his left with an invisible Dolphim at his side.

The children ran as fast as their legs could carry them into the waiting arms of their Mum and dad. There were no scoldings just happy tears as they all hugged and were more than happy just to be together again. Mum was soon fussing around them all, and then sitting down on her heel in front of Alex, she pulled out her handkerchief licked it. She started to wipe the dirt from his cheek. "Aw Mum do you have to?"

Alex then went on to say. "You know grandad looked after us, just like you and dad, you're not angry with him are you?" She pinched his nose gently, "of course not my little soldier, but where's he going now?" Mum said looking up.

Lee and dad had already started to walk in the direction grandad had taken, unaware of the Toads presence and the object of Dolphim and grandad's attention.

The evil Toad had been observing the action and felt it was time to make his getaway. Only his greed had kept him hanging on, sweating and cursing under his breath he turned the key and started the Hummers engine, he was just about to put it into reverse gear when Dolphim appeared in front of him.

His golden skin gleamed in the sunlight as he stood on top of the spare wheel on the front of the Hummer. Hiram's eyes lit up and an evil slimy grin stretched across his ugly face. "Got you, you golden lizard." He snarled as he reached into the glove compartment and pulled out a silver pistol. Dolphim leaped onto the roof his claws clattering on the steel as he taunted the Toad, running backwards and forwards on the roof.

The Toad pressed the drivers' window button to wind it down as he manoeuvred his great bulk in the seat to get his fat arm out of the window. He was trying to aim his gun at the sounds of Dolphim on the roof. His grinning face was dribbling with excitement at the prospect of a fortune soon to be his.

Then without warning, all of a sudden a mighty invisible blow struck him on the jaw through the open window. Crack! The beads of sweat flung from his head like a shower as his head shook. His eyes rolled back and his mouth fell open. On passing out, his arm dropped and the gun fell from his grip. The defeated Toad now slumped in his seat like a huge jelly.

A second later grandad materialised outside the window having tapped the talisman that hung round his neck with the ring on his finger.

"Round 2 to us I think Dolphim old chap." said grandad blowing on his fist and rubbing it with his hand. "Must say that did hurt a bit, but err, not as much as it hurt him I dare say."

"My dear friend" said Dolphim chuckling, "I feel life will be a little dull without you around, I've not had so much fun for a long time but I must get back to my family now. Once again I thank you and your family for getting young Dolphis back home to me."

"It's a pleasure sir and I am sure that we will all, be seeing each other again soon. In fact I am certain of it, especially if Alex and Dolphis have anything to do with it."

"Come and visit anytime." grandad shouted after Dophim as he bounded away.

"I will." he replied.

Just then the sound of a helicopter broke the silence as it flew over head, and as grandad moved out of the clearing to take a look, Brian and Lee strode up.

"What's going on here then?" said Lee. Grandad took them over to the hummer as the helicopter circled and started to land.

"This-- boys is the big cheese the man behind this whole thing."

"God he's ugly." said Brian, peering through the windscreen. Grandad reached in, turned the engine off and removed the keys.

A cloud of dust was being thrown up by the downdraft of air from the whirling blades of the helicopter as it settled down just in front them. The pilot shut the engine down and the doors slid open spilling out a squad of armed police and several paramedics. As the dust settled the party split, one group running towards the already captured kidnappers and the other towards grandad and the hummer. "Keep your hands where I can see them." shouted the officer in charge as they advanced.

Lee, Brian and Grandad raised their arms. Granddad shouted. "We have the ring leader here in the Hummer."

The officer in charge had already been briefed, signalling with his hand for his squad to lower their guns. "Ok Sirs lower your arms; let's take a look shall we."

He walked behind the three of them to the front of the hummer. Peering through the window he recognised the Toad from a most wanted poster back at base. Turning round and looking back at grandad he said. "Well gentlemen it looks like you've beaten us to it, please lower your arms wont you."

I am Sergeant Tony Blaze. Excuse me a moment sirs." and he turned his head and barked out his orders to his squad. "Medics you had better take a look at this slimy blob, Forbes, Slater make sure he's secure and has no hidden weapons."

"Sir." was the reply in absolute unison, as they jumped to their allotted tasks.

The sergeant held out his hand "Mr. Woody Woods I presume" Granddad shook his hand and introduced Brian and Lee. "Sergeant, there's an explosive device over there in that clearing" said grandad pointing over his shoulder. "OK sir don't worry we'll sort that out. Oh and by the way Mr. Woods our commander Mark Breen thought it might be you involved in this caper and would like to send you his regards. Apparently he was just a young inspector in Hong Kong when you assisted, shall we say, in his first case."

"Young Breeno eh, well I'll be dammed, how is he?"

"Well quite ironic really sir, this will be his last case before he retires and I think he will thank you for helping to put a nice feather in his cap sir."

"Tell him from me if he gets bored to look me up, but now I would like to get back to my family sergeant." "Will do sir, and good luck."

Granddad turned to Brian and Lee "Come on boys lets get home." He put his arms around them and they all walked towards the waiting group of family being attended to by the police and medics. As they walked Brian piped up. "Dad I thought you and Nigel where in the import export business in Hong Kong?"

"We were son, we were." Grandad winked with a cheeky twinkle in his eye and they all laughed heartily almost stumbling as they walked back towards the waiting family.

On reaching their goal everybody was in high spirits, Mia Tom and Alex rushed over to welcome them with even more hugs and kisses.

Eventually the officer in charge held his hands up and said; "Now ladies and gentlemen I am going to need some statements from all of you."

"Uhhh" was the singular reply, "but not today." he quipped. And everyone breathed a sigh of relief. "However Mr. Woods snr I would like to clear up a few things, could we just have a little chat?" and he gestured in the direction of the old Bentley.

"Of course officer." and the two of them sauntered over to Spitty, grandad sitting himself down on the step bolted to Spittys chassis.

"Now sir." said the officer opening his notebook and licking his pencil. "With all respect sir, we know you're not a fabulously wealthy man. So what was it these criminals where after?"

Granddad thought for a moment, and then he pulled down the neck of his old tea shirt and lifted out his beautiful golden dragon talisman. "This is extremely valuable and quite ancient officer."

"Yes well, that thing around your neck explains a lot Mr. Woods. The Chang brothers and Hiram Spode-Alias the Toad, where known to us as traffickers in stolen Chinese artefacts. The two brothers have been whingeing on in the back of the patrol car about a dragon. Of course we did not believe their story sir, but we've never been able to pin anything on them, until now that is. Resorting to kidnapping has cooked their goose so to speak."

Just then grandad and the policeman noticed coming from the clearing over by the Hummer a stretcher with the huge bulk of Hiram Spode on it. It was being carried by four struggling men and heading for the helicopter.

Sergeant Blaze following up the rear of the party waved to grandad as the increasing whine of the helicopters jet engine broke the silence and started to push the rotor blades faster and faster.

The Toad was at last in custody and loaded into the helicopter.

"He'll be put away for a good few years thank god." said the officer to grandad as they waved back. "I'll make out a report and get a statement from you later Mr Woods. I'm not sure I agree with your tactics, but well done anyway. Goodbye Sir."

Within a few minutes the helicopter was fully loaded and took off. Soon it was just a dot in the sky and as the dust settled again grandad looked at Spitty.

"Well old thing I think you deserve a good clean when we get home."

While the policeman walked back to the patrol car the children came running over, Alex still clutching grandad's knapsack, they cried, "grandad, grandad guess what?" as they circled him. "What is it my dragonettes" he quipped.

"Mum and dad say we can stay at Uncle Nigel's tonight." said Alex.

"Yea and Auntie Kathleen is cooking us a feast" said Tom licking his lips in anticipation. Grandad looked at his watch. "Well I guess it's too late to give our Spitty a run up the hill now children."

"Never mind grandad, there's always another day" said Mia giving grandad a consolatory hug,

The last support vehicle turned round and clattered across the old bridge disappearing from view. While the late warm afternoon sun threw shadows from the trees across the remaining family and friends readying themselves to depart. Grandad and the children climbed into Spitty and settled into their seats. Granddad started up Spitty and they gently chugged over to join the little convoy. There was Mum and dad in the old MG, Nigel in his Morgan and Lee on his borrowed Buell.

"I'm gon'na have to get this bike back to Pete" shouted Lee.

"I guess we have some stuff to pick up at Westfarland hill too" said Nigel.

"Oh don't worry about that I can get it all in my trailer" said Lee, "and besides, this little beastie go's like the wind, I bet I'll be home before you lot."

"You be careful Lee." Said Mum.

Lee pressed the starter on the bike and spun round like a dirt track rider, waving his hand as he too headed back towards the bridge and home.

Grandad climbed out of Spitty as the old Bentley gently ticked over. "You folks get on home if you want; I'm just going to refit this rear light." Dad leaned out of old no 8 saying. "If you think we are going to let you and our kids out of our sight, you have got another thing coming dad, come on I'll give you a hand." Mum nodded in agreement and added. "Are you kids ok up there?"

"Fine Mum," was the simultaneous reply.

Grandad walked over to Nigel's Morgan and leant against the cockpit. "My dear old friend," he said offering him his hand, "You are like a brother to me, thank you."

Nigel clasped his hand, "go on you old codger someone's got to keep you on the straight and narrow." Granddad smiled and he could feel his eyes filling up, he sniffed and cleared his throat, "come on give me and Brian hand to fix this light."

Grandad pulled out his handkerchief and blew his nose while walking back to Spitty; he then reached in and turned off the ignition. Mia stood up and gave him a kiss on his cheek. "Thank you grandad," she said softly. The old boy was quite over come with emotion as he bent down fumbling in his tool box looking for a screw driver. He blew his nose again making a sound like a ships fog horn, paused and said. "That's quite all right my dear, all in a days work."

Alex had settled back in his seat and was reflecting in his mind on the days events. Breathing a huge sigh he was already missing Dolphis. "I'm just going for a pee," he said opening the door. "Don't you wander off now," grandad said looking over his nose at him. "We'll be off in a minute." Alex scampered off and stood behind a crumbling wall jutting out from the old building and peed on a pile of bricks in front of him. Doing his fly's up and turning round to walk back he wondered what the dragons would be doing now deep in their cavern.

Suddenly he heard a voice that made his heart soar. "Alex, Alex." It was Dolphis.

He immediately turned round, "where are you my little friend?" his eyes searching everywhere. "Here I am," and Dolphis appeared on the window ledge of the battered building. Alex rushed over and picked him up. Dolphis danced round in his hands excitedly puffing tiny smoke rings from his nose. "I just had to tell you," he said beaming.

"The council have met and said we can visit each other any time we want, with our parent's permission of course," Dolphis added.

"That's great, Dolphis, yippee!" Alex spun round like a top laughing and giggling.

He then reached into his pocket and pulled out the matchbox.

"I'll keep this warm for you too."

"Don't you forget the charcoal and ginger beer" said Dolphis rubbing his tummy.

The pair of friends where overjoyed and celebrated the good news, but they both knew they had to say goodbye again soon. The mood changed and they both looked a little sad. Alex carefully placed Dolphis back on the window ledge. "Don't you dare cry Dolphis," said Alex waving his finger and fighting back the tears himself.

"Come on Alex! We're ready to go." His dad shouted from the waiting convoy.

"I'll see you soon Dolphis," Alex said stroking him gently, they both smiled.

"You bet Alex and give my love to Mia, Tom and grandad."

Then as Alex turned to run back, Dolphis shouted after him, "I'm going to beat you on your computer racing game next time."

"You wish, and only if you cheat," laughed Alex running off. Half way back he turned round still sort of running backwards and saw a brief flash of gold as Dolphis disappeared.

Returning to the cars Alex got back in his seat and grandad fired up Spitty, within minutes the trio of vintage machines where moving off. The children took one last look back before they trundled over the bridge, and then settled down for the journey ahead.

Soon they where heading back through the valleys winding roads. The children where very tired and the main topic of conversation was how they where going to tell Mum and dad about their new found friends but decided to cross that bridge another day. Right now the prospect of one of Auntie Kathleen's feasts was foremost in every body's minds, especially Tom.

So they all settled down, deep in thought and listened to grandad talk Spitty back down into the valley and home.

Alex had snuggled up to Mia and his eyes started to close as Spitty's rhythmic exhaust echoed off the stone walls. The late afternoon sun was as warm as toast flashing on and off on the tired faces through the trees. What an adventure they had, thought Alex dreamily. Time slowly drifted by, reality merging with dreams as Alex's mind drifted back to dark caverns and golden dragons.

Suddenly a jolt woke him as Spitty's wheel hit a pot hole. He opened his eyes and felt for the matchbox in his pocket. Had it all been a dream?

No there it was, he pulled it out and opened it. Looking up at Mia with a big grin on his face, she looked at him, smiled and gave him a big hug. They both knew their adventures in life where only just beginning.

THE END

About the Author

Born November 1950 in Guildford Surrey England. I had a very happy childhood indeed.

I think I daydreamed through most of my schooling and happily left school at 15 yrs old with no qualifications at all. Generally I ploughed through life as most of us do with all the ups and downs that that entails. I now have five children and at the last count three grandchildren.

Somehow by accident along the way I discovered my love for poetry and the written word and now enjoy writing with a passion. This is equalled only by my love of nature and all things mechanical. So I hope you enjoy this little adventure and to be sure Dolphis, Alex, Tom, Mia and of course Grandad are looking forward to sharing more of their adventures with you in the future.

Printed in the United Kingdom
by Lightning Source UK Ltd.
126154UK00003B/112/A